MARVEL

IRON MAN 3™

MARVEL

IRON MAN 3™

ADAPTED BY MICHAEL SIGLAIN

BASED ON THE SCREENPLAY BY DREW PEARCE & SHANE BLACK

PRODUCED BY KEVIN FEIGE

DIRECTED BY SHANE BLACK

MARVEL

For information, address Marvel Press, 114 Fifth Avenue, New York, New York 10011-5690.

Printed in the United States of America

First Edition

1 3 5 7 9 10 8 6 4 2

V475-2873-0-13032

ISBN 978-1-4231-7250-5

MARVEL

IRON MAN 3™

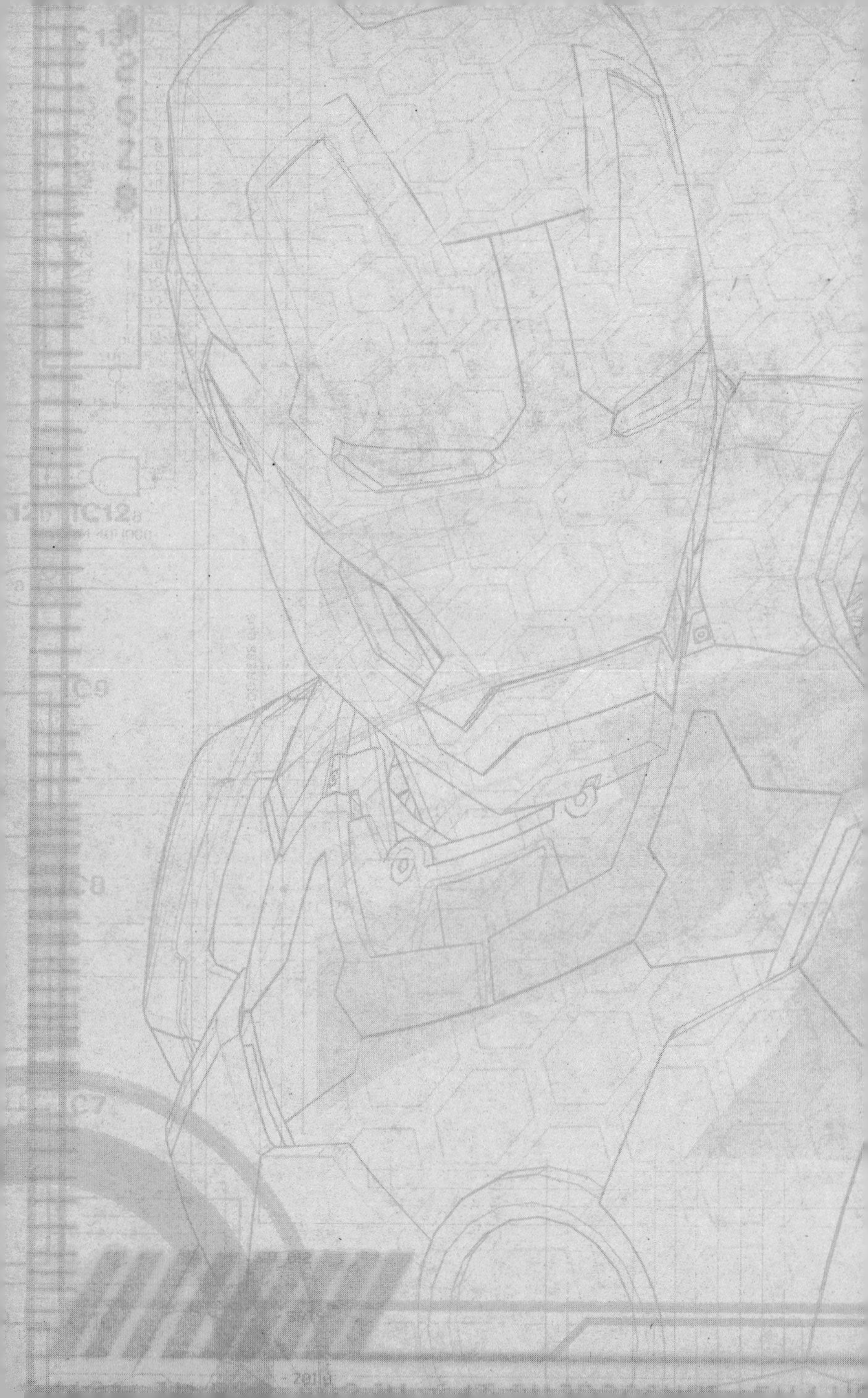

PROLOGUE

My friends, this is a story about how appearances can be deceptive.

—Tony Stark

CHRISTMAS EVE, the most magical night of the year. The night when the man in the red suit flies through the air and comes to town. But tonight, that man *isn't* Santa Claus, it's the invincible Iron Man—and this is *his* story.

CHAPTER ONE

IT WAS A BEAUTIFUL, late-December evening in Rose Hill, Tennessee. New snow had just fallen on the cold ground, and a single deer emerged from the edge of the dark forest, illuminated by the bright stars from above.

One star in particular seemed to stand out. It glowed brighter and brighter, and anyone looking up at the sky that chilly December night would think that maybe, just maybe, it was the star of Bethlehem.

But then it began to glow even more radiantly, and it started to move. Soon, it was rocketing toward that small patch of pristine snow, which was just off the main highway.

And then the star began to scream.

The "star" was actually Tony Stark, who was hurtling through the sky—or rather, out of the sky—completely out of control. His latest Iron Man armor, the Mark XLII, had been badly damaged, and he was losing power fast. He was also losing altitude. Tony Stark was about to crash into rural Tennessee.

Trying to save his Iron Man armor—not to mention his own life—Tony tried to come in for a soft landing on the snow, but it didn't work. He landed with a *thud* on the highway. His armor sparked and screeched against the pavement, then bounced back up into the air. He crashed through the forest, knocking down a few trees, and skidded through the snow and down a long hillside. That lone deer ran off in the commotion, and Tony Stark was all alone—and unable to move.

The Iron Man armor was leaking thick, black oil onto the shimmering snow. Tony looked up into the sparkling sky but heard nothing. An eerie silence surrounded him, and as the billionaire inventor and Super Hero lay on the cold ground, he thought about what had just happened. He remembered the surprise attack on his mansion in Malibu, California, and the incredible, almost never-ending explosions. He also remembered jumping into his Iron Man armor and coming to the rescue, then trying to escape.

Tony, his power supply dangerously low, had lost control of his armor, and now, here he was, crashed in the middle of a snowy field in the country. The Armored Avenger had certainly seen better days. This is not where this particular story starts, Tony thought.

Tony closed his eyes. "However smart you are," Tony said to himself, "there's nothing you can make that doesn't break eventually." As if on cue, the armor's power supply dropped down to one percent. Tony allowed himself an ironic smile at his current predicament on this, what was supposed to be one of the happiest nights of the year. Tony sighed. Right now, he was anything but happy.

This is the story of how I got my heart broken, Tony realized. I don't know where it ends, he thought. But he did know where it began. . . .

CHAPTER TWO

LONG ISLAND, New York, 1980. Unlike other kids his age, Tony Stark grew up surrounded by money. A lot of money. Tony lived in a beautiful mansion that was filled with butlers and servants, many of whom served as Tony's only friends. For, even as a small boy, Tony seemed to have a figurative suit of armor around him.

Tony was always a very smart child—a regular chip off the old block—and that was made immediately apparent by the number of science fair trophies and medals gracing the young boy's room. At just seven years old, Tony was already smarter and more creative than kids twice his age. But no matter how smart he was, there was one person who was *always* smarter, his father, Howard Stark. It was in his shadow that Tony lived.

Howard Stark was a billionaire inventor who had become internationally renowned for his futuristic inventions and innovations, as well as for being the founder of Stark Industries. But perhaps what Howard Stark was most famous for was for being a part of the Strategic Scientific Reserve—the SSR—the top-secret team responsible for creating the world's first Super Soldier, Captain America. Plus, it was Howard Stark who designed the First Avenger's iconic vibranium shield.

Tony Stark had a lot to live up to.

But not when it came to his mother. Maria Stark was a kind and thoughtful woman who nurtured the young boy. Tony always knew that this mother tried to give him the best and most normal life possible, and because of that and her warmth and compassion, Tony always wanted to make her smile. One day, while she was leaving in the car, Tony held up his hand, and it glowed, almost as if he were wearing a repulsor beam and it was about to fire. Then Tony opened his clenched fist, and several fireflies flew out from the center of his palm. Tony hadn't created a new power source, and he hadn't made a repulsor beam. But he did make his mother smile, and that was all that mattered.

Not long after that, Tony's mother died, and Tony was alone with his father. While his dad taught him many brilliant things, Tony always missed his mother and her smile.

Tony Stark the adult smiled at the thought of his mother. "But that's not where this story starts," he said to himself as he slowly lifted his head from the snow-covered ground. The air was getting colder, and the snow was beginning to collect on the Iron Man armor, but Tony remained silent and still. He closed his eyes and remembered a different woman. This woman wasn't his mother; it was an old friend who had appeared at his home hours earlier, just before the sneak attack on his mansion. Her name was Maya Hansen, and she was also a scientist. Tony had first seen her on New Year's Eve 1999. He was in Switzerland with his bodyguard and driver, Happy Hogan, and it was almost midnight . . .

CHAPTER THREE

MILLENNIAL TECH SUMMIT, Bern, Switzerland, 1999. Years before Tony Stark fought for the good of others as the Armored Avenger, he was an arrogant and cocky billionaire genius who selfishly put himself before everyone else. After the death of his father, Tony ran Stark Industries, which then specialized in creating state-of-the-art weapons for the U.S. military. But high-tech weapons were the last thing on Tony's mind at the moment. It was New Year's Eve—the millennial eve—and Tony was getting ready to celebrate the change from 1999 to 2000 with a bang.

He had just given a speech and was now enjoying himself at the cocktail party, eating and drinking and counting down the minutes to midnight. Across the room, he spotted a beautiful young scientist and made his way through the crowded reception hall to speak with her. After introducing himself, he launched into a story about his mother, but not just any story; the story about the fireflies and how, when she saw the glowing bugs fly from his hand, his mother smiled.

"The thing about my mother is," Tony continued, "she didn't smile much."

"Ugh. Seriously?" the beautiful scientist asked, not believing Tony's story.

"Hey, it's rude to interrupt," Tony said, barely missing a beat.

"But 'my dead mommy's smile is all I'm trying to get back to'? That's got to be the cheesiest pick-up story I've ever heard," the woman said.

"My mom died in that car," Tony responded.

The beautiful scientist, whose nametag read MAYA HANSEN, looked horrified. She had just put her foot in her mouth—big time.

"Yeah, eleven years later," Happy Hogan, Tony's driver and best friend, said, defusing the situation. Relieved, Maya rolled her eyes and laughed. Tony, whose nametag simply read YOU KNOW WHO I AM, smiled charmingly as a group of other convention-goers walked by.

"Tony Stark!" one of the men yelled out. "Nice speech, man!"

Tony raised his glass and smiled, then turned to Happy. "Did I have a speech? How was it?" the billionaire asked.

Simultaneously, both Happy and Maya answered.

"Entertaining," said Happy.

"Unintelligible," remarked Maya.

"A winning combo," Tony concluded. Then, reading her nametag, he said Maya's name out loud and asked to go back to her room to see her science research.

"You mean, the research that's upstairs in my hotel room, Stark?" Maya said with a shrug. "I don't know how I feel about being alone in a hotel room with you."

"Let me help you," Tony offered. "Excited."

"You're an unprincipled, profiteering mass murderer," Maya countered, referring to the weapons created by Stark Industries—everything from missiles to rocket launchers to tanks—that had been used in every major military skirmish of the last twenty years.

"You don't have to make my point for me," Tony said with a sly smile. "Look, who said we have to be alone? I hate being alone." As Tony led Maya and Happy toward the bar, they passed a young Chinese scientist who was also attending the conference.

"Dr. Wu, wassup?" Tony said to the scientist, who looked back at him, clearly surprised. "Crazy horticultural party in Maya Hansen's room. You in?"

Dr. Wu gave a wry smile as Happy began to ramble on about Y2K and the possible collapse of the all technology in just mere minutes. But as Happy talked, Dr. Wu, however, remained calm.

"To me, Mr. . . . Hogan, is it? Y2K is no more threatening for its endorsements of lazy, faux-hip three-letter contractions than for any potential it has to erase my three-thousand-year-old culture. In fact, in Beijing, the year is four thousand, six hundred ninety-eight, thank you very much," Dr. Wu said with the utmost confidence.

"Okay, you're coming. He's definitely coming," Tony said to the group as he led them over to the elevators. Just as they entered, an enthusiastic, skinny guy with a crutch and a T-shirt that read A.I.M. extended his hand. He looked scrawny and small, the complete opposite of Tony.

"Hey! What's shaking, people? It's nineteen ninety-nine. Let's party!" the new guy said to no one in particular. There was no reaction from the group. After a moment, he extended his hand again and introduced himself. "Aldrich Killian. Big fan of your work," he said.

"You know my work?" Maya asked.

"He means me," Tony assumed.

"Actually, Maya Hansen, my organization's been tracking your research since year two at M.I.T. If you both have a second . . . ?" he asked.

But Tony didn't want this skinny, nerdy guy hanging around. Just as he began to tell him that they weren't interested, Happy Hogan interjected so that Tony wouldn't have to look like the bad guy.

"What floor are you going to, pal?" Happy asked.

Killian saw his opportunity. "Ah, good question," he said. "Actually, I'm going to the ground floor." He handed each of them a business card with the logo ADVANCED IDEA MECHANICS printed on it. Killian pointed to his shirt. "A.I.M. for short," he said proudly. "I've got a proposal I'm putting together. A privately funded think tank." But Tony had had enough. He took one of Killian's business cards, scribbled something on it, and handed it back to him.

"Mr. Killian," Tony began, "I'm a billionaire and a firm believer in self-agency, which is why I implore you—go fund yourself."

Killian looked down at the business card and saw that Tony had written "Acronyms Interest Morons." Maya couldn't help but chuckle, even though she was intrigued by Killian's offer.

"Sounds interesting," Maya said. "I'm free for breakfast."

"Sure," Killian said with a smile. "See, Stark? You're not the only genius in this elevator. So, are we having a room party?"

When the elevator doors opened at the fifteenth floor, Tony, Maya, Happy, Dr. Wu, Killian, and several other scientists spilled out. Tony quickly put an arm around Killian and turned him around, leading him back into the elevator.

"You know what?" Tony said in a hushed tone. "Forget these clowns. There's a spot on the roof. Good place for us to talk in private." And with that, Tony and Killian were back in the elevator. Tony pushed R for roof, then quickly jumped out as the doors began to close. "You're gonna love it!" Tony said, finally free of his unwanted guest.

Tony turned to Maya and followed her through her door. Happy, close behind, quickly shut it before any of the other scientists could join them.

Soon, Tony and Maya sat bathed in the warm glow of a computer screen. "Wow, that's incredible!" Tony said, sounding truly impressed with Maya's research. "So, what you're doing is jacking into the genetic operating system."

"Exactly. Redirecting her body's energy," Maya said.

"And just to be sure, the 'her' you're talking about . . . she's a houseplant," Tony asked. He was looking closely at the computer screen, which showed what looked to be a normal, everyday houseplant, only with a tube attached to it. The tube was pumping some kind of liquid directly into the plant, enhancing it.

"Seriously impressive," Tony continued. "I mean, off the top of my head, I'd say sustainable crops are just the start. There are human applications, surely—"

But Maya cut him off, excited. "Exactly. Dendritic revitalization, disease prevention, even limb regrowth," she said with pride. Tony thought it sounded miraculous, but Maya said that they shouldn't celebrate just yet.

Happy was in the next room, listening to revelers count down the seconds to midnight. Getting his mind off of what he thought was sure to be the end of the world, Happy snuck into Maya's room and placed two champagne flutes and a bottle of Bollinger on her nightstand, then left. No reason that Tony and Maya shouldn't celebrate the end of the world in style, Happy thought.

"You know, you're funny," Maya said to Tony as he noticed the champagne that seemed to appear from nowhere. "You're smart; you dress nice; you have power, prestige, property . . . but the thing that is really attractive about you, that I like the most, is that you know when someone is smarter than you." Maya flashed a beautiful smile, and the two moved in close to share a kiss at midnight.

Meanwhile, Happy stood in an adjoining room and held his breath as the clock ticked down to midnight. *Three, two, one . . . Happy New Year!* But nothing happened. No Y2K bug. No chaos. No collapse of civilization as he knew it.

Just a small explosion!

Happy jumped and turned around to see a smoldering pot and, on the wall next to it, a blackened shadow of what appeared to have been a houseplant.

Happy didn't stick around to find out what had happened or why Maya's scientific research houseplant exploded. Instead, he ran from the room to find safety.

Back in Maya's room, Tony and Maya were still locked in their midnight kiss when Tony spotted an error in Maya's scientific theory. "The telomerase algorithm," Tony mumbled. Maya raised an eyebrow, and with both of them now distracted, Tony pointed to the computer screen. "I'm not an expert, but I think your glitch could be in the telomerase algorithm."

"How could I miss that?" Maya said, dumbfounded.

"Because you're smarter than me?" Tony said with a flirtatious smile. As fireworks exploded outside the room, Maya moved in close to Tony, and they resumed their midnight kiss.

As the sun began to rise over Switzerland, Happy, who was still relieved that the world hadn't ended, found Tony. As the two left the room, Tony looked over at Maya, who was already hard at work fixing the algorithm, and smiled. He wasn't sure if he would ever see her again, but he was sure she'd go far.

Slowly, Tony's mind returned to the present day and to rural Tennessee, where his Iron Man armor lay, bleeding black oil into the white snow. Today, Tony Stark was a changed man. He didn't miss the old, selfish Tony. But just a few days earlier, Tony was hard at work reversing the actions of his former self, the war profiteer. Just a few days earlier, the invincible Iron Man was on a routine mission that, unbeknownst to him, would forever change his life.

CHAPTER FOUR

EXPLOSIONS RANG out as Iron Man searched the Afghanistan desert for Stark Industries landmines that still littered the hostile land. The Armored Avenger was on a mission to destroy all of these landmines once and for all, and his mission was almost complete. The mines had been laid when Tony was a weapons manufacturer, but he wasn't that person anymore. Now, Tony Stark was a Super Hero, and he had vowed to right the wrongs of his past, even if he had to destroy each landmine one by one.

Iron Man walked a bit through the hot desert and kicked at the sand, revealing another buried landmine. Tony raised his arm, and his hand began to glow. Suddenly, a ball of energy shot out from his palm and completely encased the incendiary device. Tony lifted the energy bulb that contained the landmine high into the air, then released the energy from the device. It exploded within the energy bulb in that held it as if in a force field.

"One thousand, one hundred six down, sir. Three to go," said JARVIS, Tony's living super computer.

"Good, because all this penance is making me hungry," Tony said, and with that, the Armored Avenger located and destroyed two more mines.

There was just one left. Tony scanned the area and found it, disposing of it the same way he had the others. When the smoke and energy had dissipated, Tony lifted his Iron Man armor so he could look out across the Afghanistan border with his own eyes, rather than with Iron Man's enhanced optics.

Tony let out a long, exhausted sigh. His mission was finally complete, but Tony had only one short second to relax before the sound of an explosion caught his attention. He turned and looked off in the distance as a series of explosions rang out. Tony locked his jaw and dropped his visor into place. It was time for Iron Man to take flight.

As the sun began to rise over the Afghan border, the invincible Iron Man rocketed toward the explosions. Tony arrived in time to see U.S. soldiers in a firefight against insurgents. The American troops were attempting to enter a heavily guarded safe house and were sorely outnumbered. Iron Man landed in the middle of the wreckage and debris and made his way over to a U.S. soldier.

"Son, I hate to tell you, but your bake sale has made one giant mess," Iron Man said sarcastically.

The tired and overwhelmed soldier sighed with relief at the sight of the Armored Avenger. The soldier gave him a warm smile, then spoke into his radio to alert the rest of the troops. "All units," the soldier began, "Martini is on-site."

Tony raised his metal visor so that he could talk to the soldier face-to-face. He squinted in the sunlight to read the soldier's nametag, then addressed the young marine. "So, Lance Corporal Batters, what's the objective?" Iron Man asked.

"Capture and secure that structure, sir," Batters said. "Insurgents got some sort of vault inside. That's our target." Even though the young soldier was very happy to see Iron Man, it wasn't until just that moment that he realized that the Super Hero wasn't supposed to be a part of this mission. "If you don't mind my asking, sir, what are you doing here?" he said.

"Um, what can I say? I came for the war but stayed for the Kufta," Tony said jokingly. "So, um, what's in the vault?" he asked seriously.

"No one knows," the soldier responded.

"So it's a target because . . ." Tony asked, confused.

"Because they're guarding it. Big time," Batters said.

"My friend, that's the most illuminating distillation of the concept of war since Sun Tzu. I'm serious—copyright that." Tony said dryly. "So, what, you really need this thing?"

"On a military level, sir, I honestly don't know. But for me, I've got a six-month-old I haven't even met yet, and if I secure this vault, I might see her for Christmas," Batters said.

Tony listened to the soldier intently. He completely understood his situation and wanted to help. He wanted to see Lance Corporal Batters—and all the rest of the troops—return home to their families for Christmas. Tony lowered his visor, and Iron Man began to move toward the barricade, leaving the soldier behind. That's when Lance Corporal Batters yelled out.

"Sir, there's a sniper!" the solider warned, but it was already too late.

Iron Man was immediately hit with gunfire from three directions. *PING! PING! PING!* The bullets ricocheted off Iron Man's armor, but the gunfire didn't injure the Super Hero, it just made him mad. Iron Man quickly instructed JARVIS to recalibrate his HUD to locate the snipers. In less than three seconds, JARVIS methodically pinpointed each gunman.

Iron Man lifted his hand and pointed in those three directions. Suddenly, tiny missiles fired out from Tony's forearm armor and flew to each sniper, disabling them all. With the snipers taken out, Iron

Man kept walked toward the safe house, more determined than ever.

But the insurgents were equally determined to stop the Armored Avenger. A group of ten enemy insurgents banded together and opened fire on the hero. Iron Man simply nodded and fired a thermal emitter at the troops. Iron Man clenched his fist and activated the emitter, causing all of the insurgents' ammunition to explode. The ten soldiers dropped their weapons and retreated into the desert. Iron Man again made his way toward the safe house.

The American troops rallied behind Iron Man, and the hero led them toward the safe house. The vault was locked, but it was no match for Iron Man's repulsor beams. With a mighty blast, the steel door exploded, and Iron Man and the U.S. soldiers rushed in. But no one was prepared for what they would find inside.

There was no gold or treasure inside the vault. Nor were there weapons of mass destruction, secret plans, or insurgent leaders hiding out. Instead, the inside of the vault looked like a movie theater from back in the States. It had a large screen at one end, big, comfortable movie-theater seats, and individual buckets of popcorn placed on the edge of each chair. Everyone looked around, confused.

"Someone wanna tell me what I'm looking at?" Tony said.

The military technicians instantly did a sweep of the building, but it was clean. No bombs, no weapons, no people other than themselves. Just then, a colonel entered and surveyed the scene. His eyes locked on a remote control, and he nodded to a tech officer, who made his way over to the device. Then the colonel turned and addressed Iron Man.

"Sir, I have family in New York, and we're all extremely grateful for what you did there," the Colonel began, referring to how Iron Man and the Avengers had saved New York from Loki and his alien army a few months earlier. "But if this is what I think it is," the colonel continued, "then you never saw this." The colonel then motioned for the tech to press the "play" button. Iron Man and the rest of the soldiers watched as the screen flickered and an image formed before their eyes.

A psychedelic bombardment of twisted Americana images filled the screen. Those images dissolved into footage of various terrorist attacks from around the world until, finally, a large Chinese dragon dominated the screen. The dragon's face soon gave way to the face of a hooded figure. The camera pulled back to reveal that the figure was sprawled out on a garish throne. Kneeling before him were captured American soldiers, all of whom were clearly being held hostage by the mysterious figure. Then the figure began to speak. He began by addressing the President of the United States.

"Ah, President Ellis," the mysterious robed figure began. "You continue to resist my attempts to educate you, and now, you blew up a perfectly good safe house in the hope that I'd be there!" The figure scowled at the camera. "But no matter, today's lesson was about responsibility." Then the figure leaned forward, an evil glint in his eye.

"Question: did you know the names of all the U.S. Air Force personnel stationed in Kuwait?" the figure said threateningly. "Because I'm positive you will after my attack there." The screen abruptly cut to black.

The Colonel sprang into action, barking orders at his men, all of whom instantly followed their commander's lead.

"Okay, Sparky, you've got my attention," Tony Stark said as he snapped the visor shut on his Iron Man faceplate. He made a silent vow to find this madman—and stop him.

Iron Man's most dangerous battle was only just beginning . . .

CHAPTER FIVE

PRESIDENT ELLIS stepped up to the podium at the press conference. It was time to address the American public. The terrorist from the videotape—now known only as the Mandarin—had kept his word and attacked the Air Force base. But the president was not about to stand for any terrorist attacks, and it was time for him to make his stance known to the world—and to the Mandarin.

"My fellow Americans," President Ellis began, "when I took office, I vowed to keep America safe at all costs, and I am a man of my word. In light of the recent terrorist attack overseas, and in an effort to prevent any additional attacks either at home or abroad, I have appointed Lieutenant Colonel James Rhodes as the new Iron Patriot."

And with that, Rhodey entered the press conference and stood next to President Ellis. He wasn't in his military dress blues, nor was he wearing the gray War Machine battle armor. Instead, Rhodey was encased in his new Iron Patriot armor. It looked as if his War Machine suit had been upgraded, then repainted in red, white, and blue. The armor was reminiscent of Captain America's iconic uniform and was meant to be a symbol of strength and hope to the American public.

Cameras flashed as reporters tried to get the first official picture of President Ellis with Iron Patriot. As everyone jockeyed to get the perfect picture, the President continued his address. He spoke about the safety of America and how Iron Patriot was now the military's first and best line of defense. Beneath the mask, Rhodey smiled. He was now America's SuperHero.

* * *

Across the country, a row of big, tough-looking motorcycles lined the parking lot of a local Malibu bar and grill. And at the end of the line were two even bigger and tougher-looking rides: the Iron Man armor and the Iron Patriot armor. Both suits stood perfectly erect, as if they were guarding both the bikes and the restaurant, and inside, two old friends spoke candidly and truthfully, as they always did.

"You should see the suit," Rhodey said to Tony, referring to the new Iron Patriot armor. "It has an Evel Knievel vibe. Cooler than yours," Rhodey said with pride.

"Who knows who Evel Knievel is?" Tony said. Then, turning to a group of kids who were sitting at an adjacent table, Tony asked them if they knew who Evel Knievel was. None of them did.

Tony turned back to Rhodey, entirely satisfied with his little question-and-answer session with the kids. "Time to upgrade your references, Gramps," Tony said with a smug smile. "Try to stay relevant."

"Says the man who dyes his goatee," Rhodey

quickly retorted. Tony smiled, and the two began to discuss more serious matters.

"Truth is, Pentagon's running scared, man," Rhodey confided. "After New York, they need to look strong," he said, referring to the alien invasion that Iron Man and the Avengers had thwarted.

"So stopping the Mandarin, it's not Super Hero business?" Tony asked.

"It's *American* business," Rhodey said, correcting him. "So to do my job, if I have to be Iron Patriot, that's what I'll be."

Tony looked across the table at his friend and began to open up. "It's so easy for you," he began. "With me, it's like . . . there's the guy called Iron Man, and he's shiny and popular and . . . and amazing," he continued. "Kids love him, and he's tough, everyone knows what he stands for and . . ."

"And you don't measure up," Rhodey said, finishing Tony's thought. "You can't live up to Iron Man. I get it." Rhodey addressed his friend man-to-man. "That's what military training does for you, son. Makes it all simple. Black or white. 'Til it goes wrong, then it's just red. All over."

But by this time, Tony was no longer paying attention. He began to sweat, and his heart was racing. "Is it hot in here? I feel like I'm having a heart attack or a convulsion. Gotta get to JARVIS."

Tony rose from the table and stumbled toward the door. He tripped out into the bright sun, clutching his heart, as other patrons and bikers looked on, confused. Struggling, Tony slowly made his way past the row of motorcycles and climbed into his Iron Man armor. JARVIS instantly scanned Tony's body for injuries.

"No signs of ventricular or aortal anomaly, nor unusual brain activity," JARVIS said after reviewing the scans. "My diagnosis is that you experienced a severe panic attack."

Tony closed his eyes and thought about what JARVIS had said. They say any home, if you hide in it long enough, you'll be afraid to come out, Tony thought. That was true for him now. Tony was hiding from Iron Man—and from himself. Just then, a knock on the armor brought Tony out of his reverie. It was Rhodey, asking if his friend was all right.

"I know what I have to do," Tony said. Then he fired the suit's booster rockets. The crowd of onlookers erupted in applause as Iron Man flew off into the sky.

"JARVIS," Tony said as he soared above the ground. "Get us back to the workshop. I need to finish the new suit ASAP."

"What about date night?" JARVIS asked, but Tony ignored him as he flew toward Malibu.

Back at Stark Tower, Happy Hogan walked down a long hallway with Pepper Potts, who was on her way to a meeting that she didn't want to have.

"Ex-boss," she said to Happy. "His company's expanding, and he wants to merge R&D with us. Somehow, he got Vice President Rodriguez to vouch for him. But, back in the day, he, well, he kind of asked me out a few times," Pepper confessed. This angered

Happy, who immediately wanted to put an end to the meeting before it even began.

"Stand down," she said to the head of security for Stark Industries. "Killian's not dangerous, more along the lines of pathetic—" But Pepper stopped short as she turned the corner and came face-to-face with Aldrich Killian.

It took Happy a minute, but then he remembered Killian's face. He had seen him years earlier at that tech conference in Switzerland; only now, Killian wasn't a frail man with a cane. He was muscular and stood tall, without need of a cane or assistance of any kind. He walked with purpose, and Happy found himself trying to stand a little taller.

"Pepper!" Killian said, smiling at them both but looking directly at her. "You look great. Really, just great." Now she *had* to have the meeting . . .

Meanwhile, at his mansion, Tony, JARVIS, and Tony's DUM-E robot were testing the new Mark XLII Iron Man armor. Spread across Tony's workbench were pieces of his new experimental armor. Tony sat hard at work calibrating each piece. When he was happy with his progress, he stepped back and called out to JARVIS to record the test.

"Two forty-six pm. December twenty-first. Mark forty-two autonomous prehensile propulsion suit test with interdependent components calibrated to Mach point two. Utilize third draft of Underkofler gestures with emergency navy carrier overrides." Tony was finally ready. "Hit it," he said to JARVIS, who cranked up the Christmas music.

Thanks to miniature, high-tech implants under his skin, Tony was attempting to control his Iron Man armor by mere thought. Tony called out to the pieces of armor, but nothing happened. Then he called out again and waited. Slowly, almost magically, each piece began to levitate. Then the pieces started flying toward him. Faster and faster, each piece whipped at Tony, knocking into him and knocking him around as they began to re-form into his Iron Man armor. The only thing left was his mask, which was now flying at

Tony at ninety-nine miles per hour! Tony executed an amazing backflip just in time to catch the helmet right on his face.

The new suit worked, though it wasn't exactly how Tony had planned it. He would have to go back to the drawing board.

Back at Stark Industries, Pepper sat across from Aldrich Killian, who broke into his pitch for Stark Industries to invest in A.I.M. and in his new technology. But Pepper wasn't so sure. When she asked what, exactly, he made, his response was cryptic.

"The future," he said with a smile that intrigued her. She wanted to know more.

"After years spent dodging the President's ban on 'immoral' biotech research, my think tank now has something in the pipeline. A little idea we like to call—" he paused for effect. "Extremis."

Pepper wasn't immediately impressed. "You really need some help coming up with names," she said.

Killian stood up and rolled a marble across the table. Suddenly, the marble beeped, and they were enveloped by a huge, green, glowing hologram of constellations. These morphed into an image of the human brain. More specifically, it was a hologram of Killian's brain. Pepper was impressed but not sure of what it meant. Killian pushed back his hair to reveal nodules on his temple. He explained that there is a slot in our brains that is empty and waiting to be filled.

"Call it an upgrade," Killian said as he took Pepper's hand and led her on top of the table and into the hologram of his brain. To prove that it was really his brain, he had her pinch him. They witnessed a red flash across a section of the hologram as Killian said a quiet "Ow."

Pepper knew that Killian was on to something, but she wasn't sure what, or what the applications might be. Killian stepped down off the table and deactivated the hologram. "What if you could back up the hard drive of a living organism? Recode its DNA?"

The idea was interesting, but Pepper knew that it had the potential to be both dangerous and deadly, so she politely declined Killian's offer to team with Stark Industries.

Outside the conference room, Happy spied a burly, suspicious-looking man hanging around, apparently waiting for Killian. Happy followed the man out to the parking lot and found him sitting on Pepper's car, arguing with a bedraggled man. Happy watched from the shadows and learned that the haggard-looking man was called Taggart. He was saying something about needing more juice, but the other, whom Taggart called Savin, told Taggart that it was too soon and that he shouldn't be contacting him there. As Taggart left, Happy made his move and confronted Savin.

Their conversation became heated, with both men ready to fight, but then Killian and Pepper appeared, and both men backed off. Killian tried once more to persuade Pepper to agree to Stark Industries' investing in A.I.M's Extremis technology, but she once again declined. Killian leaned in and gave her a good-bye kiss on the cheek, and as he did, Happy made a point to remind Pepper that it was "date night" for her and Tony. Killian flashed a practiced smile, then he and Savin got in the car and drove away.

Inside the car, Savin immediately stated his dislike of Happy and Pepper, but Killian was frustrated with him for antagonizing Happy in the first place. "Savin," Killian began, "if I chose to harbor resentments, I would never have come to see a former employee who said she'd never date her boss—and who now dates her boss." Killian had a grim determination in his eyes. "Resentments will kill you. Remember that."

Pepper entered Tony's Malibu mansion and called out to him. To her surprise, Iron Man appeared in the living room. Pepper recognized that the Iron Man armor wasn't the one she was used to seeing. She guessed that it was the Mark XV, but he told her that it was really the Mark XLII. But before she could get angry with him for making so many other armors, something caught her eye—something big and brown and fuzzy. Off to the side, Pepper spied a twelve-foot stuffed rabbit wearing a big holiday bow. She smiled at the present and told Tony to come out of the suit.

But when Tony said that he wanted to stay in the suit, Pepper caught on. She walked down the stairs to Tony's workstation. Iron Man tried to stop her, but Pepper was on a mission. She snuck past the Armored Avenger and continued through the workstation to find Tony Stark watching numerous video monitors, and on each monitor was a Mandarin video. Tony was never in the suit. He was controlling it remotely. Just as she had suspected, Tony hadn't been in the suit at all. At the exact same time, the Iron Man armor waved in exactly the same way. Pepper was not happy.

Later, as Tony drifted off to sleep, he thought about his life. When I built things that hurt people, he thought, I never once had a bad dream. But ever since I started doing the right thing, it's all just been nightmares.

Tony started to twitch in his sleep. He was having a spasm, and just as Pepper tried to wake him up, a metal hand reached out and grabbed her wrist. Pepper screamed as the Mark XLII armor stood over her *without* Tony inside.

"Power down!" Tony yelled. Obeying Tony's commands, the suit immediately collapsed to the ground, smashing a night table to pieces in the process. The implants under Tony's skin must have reacted to the nightmare he was having and activated the suit. Then, when Pepper went to wake him, the suit must have been trying to protect him.

Pepper was terrified. She stood there, mouth agape, as Tony dragged the heavy iron suit out of the room.

Across town, Savin stood outside the famous Chinese theater in Hollywood. It was midnight, and his meeting with Taggart was about to begin. "Boss says if you cannot regulate, he will cut you off," Savin said matter-of-factly.

"I got this. I swear," Taggart said as he held his dogtags close. Savin noticed a single drop of silver sweat run down Taggart's face. Savin placed the briefcase on the ground and quickly walked away.

From the shadows, Happy Hogan watched the exchange. Once Savin was gone, he made his way to over to Taggart. Happy pretended to accidentally bump into Taggart, and when the two connected, Taggart dropped the briefcase, causing it to open.

Happy looked down to see a silver, inhaler-like object fall out. A puff of black smoke shot out from it upon impact. This clearly wasn't a normal inhaler. But as Happy looked up, he felt someone push into him from behind. He turned to see Savin, who immediately began to fight with Happy.

But Savin didn't know that Happy used to be a boxer, and with a mighty crack, Happy landed a punch to Savin's face that broke his nose. Happy kept his arms up as he smiled to himself—he still had it. But then he dropped his hands and his jaw went slack. To Happy's amazement, Savin's nose healed before his very eyes. Happy was dumbfounded. Then a horrible scream turned his attention back to Taggart, who was on the ground, convulsing. Taggart was overdosing on the black smoke from the inhaler.

Taggart's eyes grew wide, and for an instant, he was silent. Then his entire body exploded! Savin was knocked back by the blast. Happy raised his arms to block the force, but it wasn't enough. He, too, was caught in the blast and blown back. As Happy lay there in pain, he looked up and saw Savin walking away, his body slowly regenerating. Savin turned and smiled at the injured Happy.

People started to rush to the scene and to Happy as Savin, now perfectly fine, simply disappeared into the shadows . . .

CHAPTER SIX

IRON MAN blasted across the California night sky and landed inside the hospital where Happy had been brought after the blast. He strode through the hospital in search of the intensive care unit. When he reached it, he went directly to Happy's bedside and had JARVIS perform a full-body scan of his best and closest friend.

The nurses rushed in to prevent Iron Man from interfering with their work. Happy had been badly burned, and the doctors and nurses didn't need a Super Hero getting in their way. Iron Man may be an Avenger, but that didn't mean he was a medical doctor.

But Happy was Tony's best friend, and Tony was determined to do whatever he could to save him, even if it meant buying a new wing for the hospital. Instead, the doctors just asked that he step aside and let them work. Tony grudgingly agreed, but before he left, he noticed that Happy was clutching something in his left hand. It was dog tags. Taggart's dog tags.

Outside the hospital, Tony was immediately confronted by paparazzi and reporters asking what was going on. "Mr. Stark, insiders are telling us that all signs point to another Mandarin attack. Your reaction?" one of the reporters asked.

Tony had had enough. "My reaction . . ." Tony said with a slight pause. "Happy Hogan protected me my whole life. He's my best friend. I might've protected *him*—but I've had my hands tied by the government. I've been forced to stand down. That stops. *Tonight.*" Then he looked directly into one of the cameras and addressed the villain who has been terrorizing the world. "Mandarin, if you want a fight, you've got one. You hear me? 'Cause I'm coming for you, and either you start running or you come out to play. You want me? My address is ten thousand, eight hundred eighty, Malibu Point. I'll be waiting."

The next day, the Mandarin released a new video message. This one showed the villain sitting on a regal-looking throne inside a dark lair, a pile of fortune cookies stacked next to him. He cracked open one of the cookies and read the message inside. "Help, I'm being held prisoner in a Chinese bakery." The Mandarin rolled his eyes at the bad joke and dropped the fortune in a deep well that sat at the foot of the throne. "Someone must've been bored that day." Then the Mandarin grabbed another cookie and cracked it open. "Here's one: you will absolutely destroy Iron Man. *Whoah*, that's specific."

The Mandarin smiled a twisted, devilish smile, then leaned forward and spoke directly into the camera. "There's a funny thing about fortune cookies. They look Chinese, they sound Chinese, but *shhhh*. It's all a lie. They're an American invention like all other meaningless propaganda." The Mandarin flashed that same evil grin and warned his viewers. "Beware the Cookie Monster!" he said. Then the screen went black.

Tony sat in his house reviewing the most recent Mandarin tape. "I have no idea what I'm looking at here," Tony said as he tried to determine the Mandarin's next move and locate the villain's whereabouts. "He takes his name from an ancient Chinese war mantle meaning 'advisor to the king'—but uses South American insurgency tactics and sounds like a Midwestern preacher. There's a lot of theater going on . . ." Tony said before losing himself in thought.

He pulled up the most recent footage of the Mandarin's attack on the movie theater. After watching it and rewatching it, Tony came to an interesting realization. "No bomb parts were found in a three-mile radius of the theater," Tony said. "Tell me, JARVIS, when is a bomb not a bomb?" Tony's mind began to race.

"Bring up the thermo-signatures!" he yelled to JARVIS. But before JARVIS could react, Tony's doorbell rang. And then it rang again. JARVIS scanned the front door, but it was no one he recognized. Tony would have to answer it himself.

Tony opened the door to see a beautiful woman standing before him. "Hello, Tony. Long time no see."

"Um . . . hey, Maya," Tony said, trying to sound calm. Maya Hansen stood in his doorway with a worried look on her face.

"You remember. That's a good start," Maya said, relieved. "I, uh, need to talk to you. Somewhere private. Not here." There was a catch in her voice. It seemed as if Maya were scared.

As Tony ushered her into his home, Maya was surprised to come face-to-face with Pepper Potts, who wanted to know why a beautiful young woman was asking to see Tony. As Tony began to explain who Maya was, the woman from his past pointed at Tony's TV. On the screen was an image of Tony's mansion, with a little red dot moving closer and closer toward it. "Um . . . what's that blip?" Maya finally said.

Tony turned to look at the screen. He knew what that blip was. It was trouble—for all of them. "Incoming!" Tony yelled. "Get down!"

CHAPTER SEVEN

KA-THOOM! The missile hit Tony Stark's ultra-expensive Malibu mansion with a mighty roar and a brilliant explosion. Inside, Tony, Pepper, and Maya were thrown to the ground from the force of the blast.

As smoke filled the house, Tony called out to his Iron Man armor. It instantly flew toward him, but Tony instructed the armor to instead wrap around Pepper to protect her. Pepper was shocked to see the iron suit fly toward her and envelope her, but she was glad it did. Pepper was just mere seconds from being thrown into the side of the wall from another blast.

Tony looked through the hole in his wall to see the news helicopters morph and transform into attack helicopters equipped with Gatling guns and rocket launchers. Things were suddenly getting a whole lot worse, so Tony yelled to Pepper to keep herself and Maya safe.

Pepper didn't have time to get acclimated to the Iron Man armor or appreciate just how cool it was to wear. She had to act fast if she were to save herself and Maya before more missiles struck the mansion. Pepper tried to fire a blast from the gauntlet, but nothing happened. Then, with JARVIS' help, Pepper activated the suit's repulsors and flew toward a shocked Maya. Pepper grabbed Tony's old friend, and the two flew out of the mansion just before more missiles struck. They landed safely and watched helplessly as Tony's mansion filled with fire and smoke.

With Pepper and Maya out of harm's way, Tony could now concentrate on saving himself. He instructed the Iron Man armor to detach itself from Pepper and fly back to him. But the armor had taken on a lot of damage, and by the time it returned and formed around him, he was low on power and could not fire any repulsor blasts. It was then that the helicopters fired more missiles directly at him.

Tony took aim and fired off a missile at the closest attack copter, but instead of shooting across the sky, the missile fell to the ground in front of him with a weak thud. It was still live, but its propulsion system didn't work. That didn't stop Tony, though. He picked up the missile and, using Iron Man's great strength, flung it with all of his might toward the oncoming copter. It exploded on impact, and the aircraft fell into the Pacific Ocean.

When another copter appeared outside Tony's window, he noticed his baby grand piano sliding out of the tilted house, right for the helicopter. With quick thinking, Iron Man redirected some of the suit's power so that he could fire one short repulsor blast. He aimed his gauntlet right at the sliding piano and fired. The force of the blast sent the large and heavy piano directly into the oncoming helicopter. The impact and the extra weight of the piano were too much for the helicopter to take, and it, too, plunged into the Pacific. Iron Man was holding his own, but he didn't know for how much longer.

"JARVIS!" Tony yelled. "How are the suits?"

"Exposed, sir," JARVIS replied. This was not good. Tony couldn't chance the suits—or his technology—falling into the Mandarin's hands.

"How's the wine cellar?" Tony asked cryptically.

"Unexposed, sir," JARVIS said.

"Fine, so it's just the classics . . . can't risk them getting taken," Tony said. "Blow 'em." But JARVIS hesitated. Surely Tony couldn't be serious!

"Blow the armor!" Tony yelled to JARVIS. And JARVIS obeyed. The self-destruct mechanism in each of Tony's seven classic suits was activated, and one by one, they each exploded in their case. Tony watched in horror as the Marks I through VII detonated before his very eyes. He wasn't just destroying his armor—he was destroying part of himself in the process. He had built those suits with his own hands—they had saved him many times and, for better or worse, made him the man he was today. But Tony didn't have the luxury of dwelling on his loss. The force of the blasts had destroyed the surrounding walls, causing the sea water to pour in. Between all of the various explosions, Tony's mansion was now sinking into the ocean.

There was no time to react. As the building crumbled around him and water filled his field of vision, Tony yelled out to JARVIS.

"Give me everything in the gloves!" Tony screamed.

"Rerouting . . . *now*!" JARVIS responded, hoping that Tony's plan would work, but Tony was now buried on the ocean floor, and JARVIS was unsure of just how the gloves would help.

Suddenly, one of Tony's gauntlets rocketed off his hand, flew up and out of the water and into the air, then dived back down into the water. It found Tony, who grasped the flying gauntlet with both hands. The gauntlet then pulled Tony from the bottom of the ocean and out into the night sky. Iron Man had once again saved Tony Stark's life.

"Autopilot," Tony weakly commanded. JARVIS engaged the autopilot and informed Tony that the suit's power was now at a dangerously low two percent. Tony knew that he had to get away from where his estate once stood. He had to distance himself from everyone and everything so that he could keep his loved ones safe and focus his attention on finding the Mandarin.

Tony used the last of the suit's power to fly as far and as fast as he could. "Where are we?" he asked JARVIS.

"Five miles outside Rose Hill," JARVIS replied. That was the last thing Tony remembered before crashing down into the cold Tennessee snow. This was not how he had wanted to spend the days leading up to Christmas. . . .

CHAPTER EIGHT

THE GLISTENING SNOW fell on the prone Iron Man suit as Tony thought about the events of the day and what had brought him to Rose Hill. After what seemed like hours but was really only minutes, Tony lifted himself out of the battle-damaged suit and stared down at the lifeless friend at his feet. This was not the way it was supposed to end, he thought, so he wouldn't let it!

The Mark XLII armor had less than one percent of power, so Tony had to drag it through the cold snow in search of a phone booth. He had to contact Pepper. He needed to know that she was safe. Then he had to

Tony Stark had been hard at work on his latest Iron Man suit, which can be controlled with his mind!

The Mark XLII! The newest addition to Tony's Hall of Armor.

Rhodey's War Machine suit receives a makeover. Welcome to the age of Iron Patriot!

CEO of Stark Industries, Pepper Potts, listens to Aldrich Killian discuss his Extremis project.

Tony's best friend and new Head of Security for Stark Industries, Happy Hogan, watches Killian with unease.

The madman known only as the Mandarin threatens the lives of innocent people, including Tony and his friends.

With the Mandarin's arsenal of advanced weapons backing him, Tony's only option to defeat the villain is the Mark XLII!

Tony's "old friend" Maya Hansen comes to his mansion to catch up.

While Tony, Pepper, and Maya have an argument, the Mandarin decides to stop by as well–in the form of heat-seeking missiles!

Having survived the destruction of the mansion, thanks to the Mark XLII, Pepper wonders if Tony is ok, wherever he is.

Iron Man crashes into the woods of rural America. Tony's Mark XLII suit is leaking oil and is heavily damaged.

When Tony drags his suit to a nearby shed, he meets Harley. Like Tony, Harley is a scientist and offers to help fix the Iron Man armor.

With no tools, JARVIS, R&D room, Pepper or Happy to help him, Tony was all on his own. But he would fix his suit and defeat the Mandarin, no matter what.

tell her not to trust anyone, even Maya. Most important, he had to let her know that he was still alive.

Inside the phone booth—which was not as close as Tony had hoped—he propped up the Iron Man armor and left a message for Pepper. He wasn't sure when she would get it, but he had told her that he was stranded in the middle of rural Tennessee and that he was safe. He also told her that he would be out of touch for a few days. He needed this time to fix his armor—and to find the Mandarin.

As Tony hung up the phone, he spied an old shed about a hundred yards away. He made his way to the shed and peered in the window. He saw a workbench and tools—just what he'd need to begin fixing his armor. Exhausted, Tony kicked open the door, dragged the armor onto a large workbench, and collapsed into a deep sleep.

Tony woke with a start and stared at the Iron Man helmet on the workbench across from him. "Sleep when you're dead, right, buddy?" Tony said to the empty metal armor with a sigh. "That won't be long now if I don't get you fixed," he said, tired but determined. This was more than just armor for Tony. In a way, it *was* Tony. He had to get back to work.

To his surprise, JARVIS managed just enough power to reply. "I—I actually think I need to sleep now, sir."

"Hang on! Do not—" Tony started to yell, but it was too late. JARVIS had powered down. The suit was out of power. Tony slammed his fists on the table and let out a primal scream of frustration.

"That sounds pretty bad, sir," a small voice said from behind him. Tony spun around to see a boy standing in the shed's doorway. He looked about nine years old.

"Oh, hey. Didn't see you there, kid," Tony said as he pulled a tarp over the Iron Man armor.

"What are you doing?" the boy inquired.

Tony had to think of a quick lie that would fool the child. "I—your dad said it was okay for me to use his shed for a little while," Tony fibbed.

"That's weird," said the boy, "because my dad is dead."

"Ah, well, I didn't say *when* he told me that, which was actually before he died," Tony continued to lie.

"You're in a lot of trouble, mister," the boy began, but Tony cut him off. He didn't have time to deal with a kid right now.

"Well, first, no, I'm not, because I'm just a friendly hobo. And second, what century are you from, Huck Finn? Who even says 'mister' anymore?" Tony said, returning to his usual self.

"If you'd let me finish," the boy began, "I was going to say 'Mister Stark.'" With that, the boy held up the late edition of the evening paper. The headline read MANDARIN ATTACK: STARK DEAD. Tony grabbed it out of the boy's hands and instantly scanned the article.

"No way!" the boy yelled. "Iron Man is here!"

"Yeah, yeah. You got me. It must be a pretty big deal for you—" Tony began, but the young boy cut him off.

"No, you're Tony Stark. You're boring," he said very matter-of-factly. "This is Iron Man!" he yelled. Tony turned to face the boy and found him standing next to the Iron Man armor under the tarp on the floor beside him. Tony really didn't have time for this.

"Look, kid, now's not the time for an existential debate. There's some stuff I need." Tony kneeled down to the boy's level. "Can you help?" he asked.

"Sure, but what's in it for me?" the boy replied. This is a kid after my own heart, Tony thought. He scanned the room and noticed a bunch of science trophies and medals on the wall.

"What's your name, kid?" Tony asked.

"Harley."

"Okay, Harley, and what's the name of the kid that bullies you?" Tony asked with sincerity.

"Wait—how did you know about EJ?" Harley said, confused.

"Because you're smart," Tony replied. "People are always trying to beat up on smart guys like us." Tony pressed a button on the Iron Man armor and extracted a small silver capsule that he then tossed to Harley.

"Cool!" the boy exclaimed. "How does it work?"

"There's a button on the side," Tony said, his tone now serious. "Don't use it near anyone's eyes unless you want to go to jail for ten years." The boy nodded.

"Now, you in?" Tony asked. Harley nodded again, and Tony returned the gesture. "Good. Write this down," he said. "I'm going to need a laptop, a digital watch, a cell phone, some kind of metal spring, and one large tuna fish sandwich. And no tweeting. Think you can handle that?" Tony asked.

"Sure," Harley replied. "But what are you doing *here*?"

"Funny you should ask, Harley," Tony said. "I'm here to find a dead guy."

CHAPTER NINE

PEPPER POTTS stood at the edge of the wreckage of Tony Stark's Malibu mansion. Everything was in ruins, and what wasn't destroyed or in a shambles was now under the sea. Among the debris and ash, far away from the first responders and emergency medical technicians, was the face of Iron Man. More specifically, it was the helmet of Tony's now-destroyed Mark IV suit.

Pepper made her way over to the dented Iron Man helmet and picked it up. She held it tenderly and lifted it to her forehead, hoping that Tony, wherever he was, was okay. Suddenly, a light flashed inside the helmet. Pepper looked around, and when no one was watching, she put it on.

A retina scan confirmed that Pepper was really Pepper, and that's when she heard Tony's voice—it was Tony's message from when he called from the phone booth. He hadn't called her cell—he called and left a message for her on his armor! Pepper's eyes began to tear up as she listened to Tony's voice asking her if she was okay and telling her not to trust anyone. But to someone watching from afar, they saw a beautiful woman wearing the Iron Man helmet. What a strange sight *that* must've been.

When Pepper removed the helmet, she saw a group of reporters heading her way. One overeager reporter ran right up to her. "The question that right now nobody can answer is, where is Tony Stark?" But Pepper didn't answer him either. Instead, seeing Maya exit a nearby ambulance, she made her way over to it.

The EMTs wanted Maya to go to the hospital to get checked out, but she refused. She felt fine, but the medical technicians disagreed. Just then, the Mark IV helmet rolled directly in front of their feet as a voice yelled out, "Helmet bomb!"

Everyone scattered, and Pepper, who was now in her car, screeched to a halt in front of Maya and yelled for her to get in. Within seconds, the two were speeding away.

"Helmet bomb?" Maya asked.

"I had to improvise," Pepper said with a smile. Then she turned to Maya, suddenly serious. "Tony's alive," Pepper said. "He asked me to get you someplace safe."

"Really?" Maya said, wondering what his plan was.

"No, he said to stay away from you," Pepper confessed. "He said you're poison or something."

Maya was shocked. "I said, like, three words to him! Who is he, Svengali?" she said. A moment passed between them as they drove in silence. Then Maya spoke up again. "But you and me—we're okay?"

"If I lost sleep over every one of Tony's ex-girlfriends, I'd be awake for the next year. We're okay,"

Pepper said. "But you need to bring me up to speed. Tony said you were a botanist?"

"Figures," Maya said, not surprised that Tony got her job wrong. "What I am is a biological DNA coder running a team of forty out of a privately funded think tank. But sure," she said with an exasperated sigh, "botanist."

"Biotech, huh?" Pepper said, impressed. Growth industry. "There's a guy I've been talking to, his stuff's amazing. Do you know Aldrich Killian?"

"Of course," Maya said. "I mean—he's my *boss*. And that's my *stuff*!'

Pepper's jaw dropped at the admission. As the car sped on, she realized they had a lot to talk about.

CHAPTER TEN

NIGHT HAD FALLEN on Rose Hill as a mysterious stranger stepped out from the shadows and onto Main Street. Clad in a Stetson hat, a borrowed army jacket, and cowboy boots, the figure stopped and looked at his reflection in the mirror.

Tony *wasn't* impressed. These weren't the designer clothes he was used to; they were Harley's father's clothes that he was wearing to blend in with the locals. Even still, Tony stuck out like a sore thumb.

Not liking the hat, Tony lifted it off his head and tossed it away. Harley, who had now joined him, nodded his approval. But Tony still had some problems with his appearance.

"You know, when you said your sister had a watch, I was kinda hoping for something a little more . . . grown-up," Tony admitted as he raised his wrist to reveal a little girl's plastic pink watch.

"She's six," Harley retorted. "What did you expect? A Rolex? Anyway, it *is* a limited edition," he said as he led Tony to the end of an alley. "This is the place you were asking about. They call it the Shadow Wall."

At the edge of the alley, burned onto the broken brick wall, were five ashen shadows that looked vaguely human. The image sent a chill down Tony's spine.

"Can you tell me what happened?" he asked.

"I guess . . ." Harley said slowly as he collected his thoughts. "This guy named Chad Davis lived around here. Won a bunch of medals in the army. But one day, folks say he went crazy . . . made, you know, a bomb." Harley stopped speaking for a second before adding, "Then he blew himself up. Right here."

"Six people have died, right?" Tony confirmed. "Davis included?" he asked.

Harley again nodded, then fell silent before beginning again. "Afterward, people in town, they'd go on about these shadows, saying how they're like the marks of souls going to Heaven. Except the bomb guy," Harley said, referring to Chad Davis. "He's going to the *other* place, on account he didn't rate a shadow. That's why there's only five."

Tony took a deep breath and let Harley's words sink in. As he did, he lifted a repulsor lens from his coat pocket and turned it over in his hand. Looking to the human-shaped shadows on the brick wall, Tony started turn the lens over faster and faster. And as he did, his breathing got heavier and heavier. This worried Harley.

"Hey, you okay?" Harley asked. "Can I get you something? Do you need to sit down?"

"I just . . . kid, you're going to have to stop talking. Give me a minute here," Tony replied. But neither Tony nor Harley was prepared for what happened next.

With a whoosh of snow, two quad motorbikes zoomed past them, kicking up snow in their wake. As they passed, a boy on one of the bikes slapped Harley on the back of the head.

"Yo, Harley! Who's that, your boyfriend?" It was EJ, the boy who was bullying Harley.

But Harley saw this as his opportunity to finally show up his tormentor. "You know who this is? it's Tony Stark!" Harley yelled. Beaming, Harley turned to Tony, but instead of seeing the hero who was Iron Man, Harley saw a fragile man was now down on the ground, breathing hard, and in the grip of a panic attack.

"Tony Stark's *dead*!" EJ yelled back. "Just like you're gonna be at school!" EJ then revved his bike and kicked more snow in Harley's face before speeding down Main Street.

"What was *that*?" Harley yelled to Tony. "You're supposed to be a Super Hero! You didn't do *anything*! Why are you so weird?" Harley was genuinely confused.

Once Tony calmed down and caught his breath, he said, "Sorry you saw this. I don't know what's going on.

Look, I need one last favor. The bomb guy's mother, Mrs. Davis. Do you know where she might be?"

"Um, yeah. Sure. Where she always is," Harley said. Then he raised his arm and pointed to the end of the street, to Walker's Bar.

CHAPTER ELEVEN

TONY STARK stood outside Walker's Bar, nervous. After his most recent panic attack, he wasn't sure he could handle anything without his Iron Man armor. Inside the suit, he was safe and protected and could defend those around him. Now, he couldn't even come to the aid of a nine-year-old boy. With all of these thoughts swirling through his mind, he almost didn't notice the beautiful woman walking out of the restaurant. And if it wasn't for the fact that she dropped her scarf in front of him, he wouldn't have noticed her at all.

As Tony picked up the scarf and handed it back to her, the two locked eyes. She stared directly at him—she recognized him! But when she brushed back her hair, she revealed a scar on her cheek and a missing earlobe. Now it was Tony who found himself unable to look away. Knowing he was busted staring, he instantly tried to cover.

"Nice haircut," he said awkwardly.

"Nice watch," she retorted, noticing his plastic pink watch.

"It's a limited edition," he said, without missing a beat.

"I don't doubt it," she said with a smile. The two flirted a little more, then as she made her way down the street, she turned back to see if Tony was still looking. He was.

CHAPTER TWELVE

INSIDE WALKER'S BAR, Tony sat at a table and looked up at a television that was airing a news alert.

"In a broadcast from the White House this afternoon, recently elected President Ellis pledged to neutralize the terrorist known as the Mandarin," the anchor said. The report then cut away to the president.

"You elected me on a simple platform—that I defend America at all costs," President Ellis said. But some of the patrons didn't agree.

"It's not us he defends, it's the fat cats who line his

pockets!" the bartender yelled to Tony, who happened to be the closet person to him.

"Yeahhh . . . I always figure, it's a really hard job—I wouldn't want it," Tony replied.

"Sure, but I wouldn't wanna be one of them fishermen, neither, on account o' that oil tanker went belly-up, sliced the coast. Not a single fat cat saw a courtroom. That ain't defending America."

Tony turned his attention back to the television and listened as the news anchor continued. "Central to President Ellis's counterattack on the Mandarin is Colonel James Rhodes, or as the press is now calling him—Iron Patriot."

"Yeah, that's not painting a target on your back," Tony said aloud to no one in particular about Rhodey's new armor.

Just then, a bar patron came up to Tony because he recognized him, but Tony pretended he wasn't really Tony Stark. The patron believed him, then Tony walked off to get the information he was in there for.

"Mrs. Davis," Tony said to the woman in the corner. "Can I take five minutes of your time?" But Chad Davis's mother thought that Tony was from the government, and she wasn't interested in speaking with anyone else from there. Tony told her that he wasn't a government agent, but she didn't seem to care.

"FBI, army—it's all the same, right? Listen, I brought your file. Now let my boy rest in peace," she said. Tony looked down and saw a think manila envelope with the words CHAD DAVIS MEDICAL HISTORY embossed across the top. Beneath that were the letters M.I.A., stamped in red ink, which stood for MISSING IN ACTION.

"Mrs. Davis, I don't know who you're expecting, but it's not me," Tony confessed.

"The government people called and said you needed this," she said, referring to her son's file. But Tony wasn't from the government, nor were there any government agents around. This worried Tony, but he kept on talking. He had to learn more about what was going on.

“No. Wrong guy,” Tony replied. “I came here about your son. About what happened.”

Mrs. Davis took the file back then told Tony that her son would’ve never done the things that people said he did. And he would never have harmed innocent people.

“I believe you,” Tony said. “But tell me one thing—how did he end up back here?”

Mrs. Davis wondered if she could really trust the man in front of her. She decided she could, and leaned forward and opened her son’s file. “My son was real brave, sir,” she began. “But when he came back here, he was AWOL. He saw something that freaked him out so bad that he ran on home. Wouldn’t even talk about it,” she said sadly.

Tony picked up the folder and began to flip through it. He saw pictures of soldiers, one of whom caught his attention. Under the picture was written the soldier’s name: TAGGART. That was the same name that was on the dog tags that Tony found clutched in Happy’s hands. This was definitely *not* a coincidence.

Tony then took a photo out of his pocket and slid it across the table to Mrs. Davis. It was of the attack at the movie theater.

"Last week in L.A.," Tony said, referring to the picture. "Same sort of thing. Ten people ripped apart by an explosion. But in this photo, I count only nine blast shadows. That bothered me. Then I thought, what if maybe, just maybe, the tenth person *was* the explosion."

Tony reached across the table and gently took Mrs. Davis's hand. "I don't think your son killed himself," he continued. "I think someone turned him into a bomb . . . and he went off too soon." Then he looked the woman in the eyes. "It wasn't his fault."

"Forgive me for sayin', sir, but that sounds awful science-fictional," Mrs. Davis said. "You got any kind of proof?"

As if on cue, the scarred woman whom Tony had encountered earlier in the night walked back into Walker's Bar. Her eyes locked on Tony. "Ma'am, I think it just walked in," Tony said as the woman made her way to their table.

The woman, whose hair was down to obscure her scarred face, lifted an FBI badge from her pocket and said her name was Agent Brandt. "Mr. Stark, I'll ask you to stay calm and put your hands on the table," she said with a slight inference of threat.

"Whatever this is," Tony said, "Let's take it outside. It's not about these people."

Just then, one of the locals walked up to them and asked what was going on. Brandt said that it was none of his business and that Tony was under arrest.

"Well, that *sounds* like my business," the local man said. Then he pulled out his badge. He was the town sheriff, and his partner was right next to him. "See, if you're FBI," the Sheriff said, "why wasn't I informed that you'd be actioning a takedown in the town under my jurisdiction?"

Tony quickly joined in, hoping to keep everyone calm. "Sheriff, that's a great question. Perhaps we can address it somewhere less populated," he suggested.

But Brandt continued her façade. "This man is a suspected threat to Homeland Security, Sheriff—that kind of info is probably a little above your pay grade," she said with a condescending tone to her voice.

"Fine. So how's about you get on the horn to Homeland and upgrade me. I'll wait," the Sheriff confidently retorted.

"Okay, I hear you," Brandt said with a sigh. "My bad. But could I borrow your gun?"

"I don't have a gun," the Sheriff admitted. "And even if I did—" That was all she needed to hear. Before the Sheriff could continue, his eyes grew wide in shock as Brandt's hands began to glow and pulse with energy.

Suddenly, the metal FBI badge in her hand grew red-hot and began to melt. The two sheriffs and Tony looked on in disbelief, and that's when Brandt made her move. She used her energy hands to attack both the sheriff and his deputy, dropping them both to the floor in a matter of seconds. They never stood a chance against her.

"Not here!" Tony yelled as he ran out the door, hoping that Brandt would follow him rather than endanger everyone else in the restaurant. Luckily for them, she did. Brandt followed Tony outside and moved in for the kill.

"Please, Mister Stark," the woman with the glowing hands said. "Do you really think there's any point in running?" Just then, a gunshot rang out. Then two more. Both Tony and Brandt ducked for cover as gunfire exploded around them. The locals inside the restaurant had coming rushing out, guns drawn, looking for the woman who had attacked the sheriff and his deputy. But their appearance only angered Brandt more, causing her to turn her attention—and her pulsing energy hands—to them.

As Brandt confronted the locals, more gunshots echoed through the snowy streets. These were from Savin's gun. He had now joined the fight outside the restaurant. There was panic and chaos on Main Street, with frightened people running for cover from the mayhem.

Savin, whose left hand also glowed with energy, fired a gun at Tony with his right. Tony jumped away just in the nick of time, but then looked up to see that both of Savin's hands were glowing. Using his enhanced powers, Savin melted a piece of metal off a nearby water tower and threw it at Tony.

The water tower was now unstable, and it buckled and collapsed to the ground, barely missing EJ and his motorbike. But when the tower hit the ground, the casing exploded, and hundreds of gallons of water flowed through the street, completely covering a now helpless EJ. The kid who had bullied Harley was now fighting for his own life.

Shocked at the events unfolding around him, Harley started to run toward Tony, but he was too late. Savin grabbed him by the collar and started dragging him down the center of Main Street for all to see.

Meanwhile, Brandt, whose her hands were still glowing with energy, reached up and grabbed onto some low-lying power lines. Her radiating hands snapped the live wires, and electricity shot through her body. But rather than being hurt or burned by the electricity, Brandt simply absorbed the energy, making her more and more powerful. Then she started walking toward Tony.

Tony looked around at his oncoming attacker and the devastation around him, and his breathing got heavier and faster and he grew more and more worried. Brandt and Savin were here for *him*, he thought. All of this damage and destruction was *his* fault. He may not have the Iron Man suit, but he wasn't going to go down without a fight. As Brandt approached him, Tony struck his best Iron Man pose and held up his right hand, as if he were still wearing a gauntlet with a repulsor beam. Brandt just laughed. But then, much to her surprise, Tony pulled back his sleeve to reveal a makeshift repulsor beam! He fired it at point-blank range, hitting Brandt squarely in the chest and knocking her back several hundred feet. Then Tony yelled out to Harley.

"Remember what you're going to use on bullies!" he yelled. Thankfully, Harley knew exactly what he was talking about. He reached into his bag and produced the small silver capsule that Tony had given him back at the shed. Harley held the device up by Savin's eyes. Then, closing his own eyes tight, Harley pressed the button, which sent out a blinding white light in all directions. The flash momentarily disoriented Savin, causing him to drop Harley to the ground. Harley ran as fast as he could toward Tony.

That's when the two of them saw Mrs. Davis leaving the restaurant. She wanted to get out of there just like everyone else, but Savin saw her go. He quickly rose from his knees and followed her, and within seconds, she was cornered.

Tony ran to her aid, but Brandt merely laughed. He raised his hands to fire energy beams at her, but then he was struck with a great, albeit dangerous and crazy, idea. He quickly removed the repulsor tech from his space suit and flung it at Mrs. Davis. She caught it, but she was very surprised.

As Savin laughed, he heard a weird rattling sound from behind him. He looked over his shoulder to see a piece of metal shaking uncontrollably. With extreme force, it detached itself from its bindings and flew straight at—and right through—Brandt, knocking Savin to the ground. The metal then landed harmlessly on the piece of repulsor tech in Mrs. Davis's hands.

She looked to Tony, who shot her a quick smile. "It's magnetic," he said, referring to the repulsor tech. But they didn't have time to celebrate. Brandt would soon use her powers to re-form. But before they could do anything else, they heard a scream from down Main Street. A woman stood over the unconscious body of EJ, Harley's bully. EJ had been caught in the wave of water from the water tower collapse and wasn't waking up. The woman was beginning to panic.

Tony and Harley sprang into action and ran down the street. Reaching EJ, Tony frantically began to dismantle the repulsor tech around his heart. As a crowd formed around them, Tony used his own heart to jumpstart EJ's. By creating a makeshift defibrillator with his own repulsor chest piece, Tony was able to shock EJ's heart and revive the boy. As the crowd cheered, Tony turned to Harley.

"You're going to have to look after him now," he said to his companion. "I'll call you later." And with that, Tony picked up the cowboy hat that he had thrown off his head earlier, ran to Savin's car, and drove off into the night. Brandt and Savin would give chase soon enough, so Tony had to put as much distance between himself and them as possible.

Minutes later, Savin's body re-formed itself, just like it had done after the blast outside the movie theater. Main Street was now filled with police and emergency personnel, so Savin kept to the shadows. He made his way over to where Brandt had landed and saw that she, too, was re-forming, only at a much slower pace. He lifted his cell phone and called it in.

Aldrich Killian picked up his ringing cell phone and spoke to Savin. "Brandt's down but not out," Savin told his boss. Then Savin saw something small glisten in the snow. He knelt down and lifted up Tony's small repulsor lens. It must've come loose when he blasted Brandt, he thought. He instantly told Killian what he had found. Killian smiled at the fact that Iron Man's armor was no more.

"This is a good day," the head of A.I.M. said to Savin with an evil smile.

CHAPTER THIRTEEN

WITH THE DAWN came a new videotaped message from the terrorist known as the Mandarin. This was the first time he had appeared since the destruction of Tony Stark's mansion and, for all the world knew, the death of Tony Stark himself.

In the latest video, the Mandarin produced an old rotary phone—one without buttons in which people had to manually turn a dial—and a handgun. Looking directly into the camera, he spoke without inflection. "The next lesson is about accountability," the villain said cryptically.

Then the message went black, and the world got a little more frightened. No one knew where or when the Mandarin would strike next.

CHAPTER FOURTEEN

A HUGE FIREFIGHT was under way in the desert of Pakistan. Insurgents were firing automatic weapons on a metallic Super Hero, only it wasn't Iron Man—it was Iron Patriot.

Rhodey, inside the Iron Patriot armor, returned fire in an effort to stop the insurgents and learn the whereabouts of the Mandarin.

During the battle, Rhodey's cell phone rang. The armor displayed the caller ID, which read MARTINI. It was Tony! The armor allowed Rhodey to answer his friend's call immediately.

"You're alive!" Rhodey said with relief. "Where are you?"

Tony was sitting in a phone booth flipping through the file on Chad Davis. He began telling Rhodey about the attack in Tennessee, but then he stopped cold. He stared into the glass reflection and saw the word A.I.M. staring back at him. He looked down at Chad's file and saw that it really said M.I.A. The reflection in the glass had reversed the letters and given Tony a clue as to who was behind everything.

Without wasting time, he asked Rhodey for his secure, top-secret computer access code to A.I.M. Rhodey reluctantly agreed, and Tony hung up. He had to find a computer, and he had to get to work—fast!

CHAPTER FIFTEEN

TONY DROVE AROUND in Savin's sedan looking for some kind—any kind—of technological assistance. But he found nothing, so he would just have to improvise.

After he drove past a sign for a local beauty pageant, a lightbulb went off in Tony's head. He quickly pulled over and called the police. He told them that someone had called in a bomb threat to the beauty pageant. He then hung up the phone and waited, and in just three minutes, the parking lot was full of police cars, fire trucks, and news vans. When no one was looking, Tony snuck out of his car and into the back of a news van. The computers in the back of it—as well as its satellite upload capabilities—could tell him everything he needed to know about A.I.M.

But as he was searching the internet, Tony was interrupted by the van's driver, a man named Gary who just so happened to be Tony's number-one fan. He had even cut his hair and grew a goatee like Tony's. A fanboy was the last thing Tony needed right now . . . or was it? Tony decided that having his biggest fan here was actually an asset. Gary could help Tony, and right now, Tony needed as much of that as he could get.

The two men scoured the internet until they found top-secret A.I.M. files, including a classified interview with Chad Davis. "Okay, tell no one," Tony instructed Gary, who immediately nodded agreement as they watched the interview. Continuing their search, Gary noticed that many of the other interviewees were famous sports stars—and all extreme sports stars at that.

"These names," Gary said. "I count one, two, three—all dead." With mounting dread, Tony and Gary continued their search until they got to a locked file. Its security was too much for Gary to break, but not for Tony. In a matter of seconds, he was in, though he almost wished he weren't. The footage in the last file showed six men and women marching in a line toward an operating theater. And standing just outside the theater, welcoming everyone in, was Killian Aldrich.

"Oh, great, *you're* here," Tony said, referring to Killian. Then Tony turned up the volume to hear what Killian was saying.

"I promise you, friends," Killian began. "Looking back, there is nothing better than the memory of a glorious risk you prudently elected to forego. This day—today—is your glory." The six volunteers were then given a special serum that made them convulse with pain. Then there was silence. Then all six people exploded, leaving only vague, human-like shadows burned into the wall behind them. Tony and Gary recoiled in horror.

"I was wrong," Tony said aloud to Gary, but really more to himself. "He doesn't want them to explode. The ones that got hot are failures, and he's covering them up." Then Killian began to speak again on the video.

"People, is this really the best we can do?" he yelled at the doctors and scientists present. "One in twelve is not a success rate!" Gary and Tony looked at each other, disgusted and disturbed.

CHAPTER SIXTEEN

IN A ROOM at the Southwestern Hotel not too far from where Tony's Malibu mansion used to be sat Pepper Potts and Maya Hansen. The two were discussing all of the events of the last few days, from Pepper's meeting with Killian, to the attack on Tony, to Tony's cryptic message not to trust anyone. Just as Maya was telling Pepper about the A.I.M. think tank, there was a knock on their door announcing room service. But when Pepper opened the door, she was shocked to see Killian standing before her. And that's when Pepper realized that Maya was still working for

A.I.M. Tony had been right: she shouldn't have trusted Maya!

Pepper tried to make a break for the door, but Killian was too fast. He ran in front of her, grabbed her arm, and threw her across the room. Pepper landed on the bed, and when she looked up, Killian was already standing over her, holding an Extremis inhaler. Killian tried to use the inhaler on Pepper, but she turned away at the last second, causing the black smoke to hit the wall with a strange sizzle. Now Pepper was *really* worried . . .

In the news van, Tony and Gary were watching more footage of A.I.M.'s Extremis experiments. The latest tape showed Brandt, who was missing an arm and had scars crisscrossing one entire side of her body. "If it's all the same, doc," Brandt said, "I wanna keep the face. I earned it."

Just then, the cell phone that Tony had taken from Harley began to ring. It was Harley, who had an update on JARVIS. The Iron Man armor was slowly starting to repair itself, and JARVIS now had a fix on the Mandarin—the source of the villain's video messages had been pinpointed to Miami.

Tony said a quick good-bye to Gary and jumped back in Savin's car. He was now on his way to the Sunshine State.

CHAPTER SEVENTEEN

IRON PATRIOT landed in front of A.I.M.'s headquarters. His helmet slid up to reveal the face of Lieutenant Colonel James Rhodes. Rhodey was responding to an urgent call, but when he arrived, no one was there to greet him, which he found odd. Rhodey cautiously made his way inside the headquarters, but found that the building also was deserted. He started to scan the area when the sound of gunshots echoed through the building. He slid his helmet down to protect his face and armed his shoulder-mounted Gatling gun.

Slowly, Iron Patriot made his way through the complex until he found the source of the gunshots. It was Savin. He was trying to get Iron Patriot's attention, and it had worked—Iron Patriot had walked right into a trap!

Savin pressed a button on what looked like a small remote-control device, and Iron Patriot's armor buzzed. Then it went into lockdown mode. The suit couldn't respond to Rhodey's commands, but Rhodey wasn't about to activate the emergency protocol to escape. It was a standoff.

No matter, Savin thought. *If he won't come out willingly, we'll pry him out.*

Tony drove through the bright Florida sunlight and turned into the local hardware store. If he were going to confront the Mandarin, he would need some provisions. It was bad enough that he didn't have his Iron Man armor. If he could just pick up a few things, he might at least have a fighting chance.

Inside the store, Tony quickly and methodically threw item after item into his cart, taking exactly what he needed but nothing more. During his shopping spree, he tried to call Rhodey, but his friend didn't answer.

As he was checking out, the cashier was watching a news report on her cell phone. The report said that the president of Stark Industries was now missing. Tony froze in his tracks. Pepper Potts was the president of Stark Industries, and now she was in danger. The Mandarin or A.I.M. or both were going after her to get to him.

"It ends here," Tony said with grim determination as he exited the store.

CHAPTER EIGHTEEN

TONY PARKED his car a few hundred yards away from the Mandarin's compound. But the villain's home didn't look like a terrorist stronghold. Instead, it looked like a rock star's mansion. It was big and extravagant and could have easily belonged to Tony.

Tony took out guard after guard with makeshift Tasers and homemade knockout gas as he made his way toward the house. "I can run away all I like," Tony said as he zapped one of the approaching guards who yelled for him to halt. "But at the end of the day, I can weaponize anything." Tony eliminated that guard, then two more. He was getting closer and closer to the Mandarin himself. He just hoped that his do-it-yourself weapons would be enough.

Once inside, Tony silently crept toward the Mandarin's stateroom. His heart was racing and his breathing was labored, but he continued on. He was close to confronting the Mandarin and would do whatever it took to stop him. This evil terrorist was responsible for the deaths of innocent civilians, the hospitalization of Tony's best friend, the destruction of Tony's home, and the disappearance of his girlfriend. One way or another, Tony wasn't going to let him escape.

Tony entered the Mandarin's stateroom and found the villain asleep on a bed. Tony slowly made his way over to the bed, being sure not to make a sound. He had the element of surprise on his side, and he was going to need it.

Tony stood before the sleeping villain and prepared to strike, but before he could do anything, he was slammed on the back of the head by a mighty blow. Tony collapsed and fell, unconscious. Standing behind him with glowing energy hands was Brandt, an evil and satisfied smile across her face.

Tony awoke in a dreary basement prison cell. He winced as he ran his hands across the welt on the back of his head. He looked around, surveying the scene. His situation had not improved. All of his makeshift weapons were gone, and he was surrounded by armed guards.

Across from him, hard at work in what appeared to be a mini-laboratory, was Maya Hansen. Various plants—half of which were connected to tubes and computer wire—filled her workspace. But before Tony could speak, Killian walked in, followed by Pepper, who was strapped to a gurney.

Tony knew that Killian and A.I.M. were connected to the Mandarin, but he hadn't known just how closely they were connected until just then. Clearly, they were working together, but to what end? he wondered. The Extremis serum was slowly being used to create a super-human army, but for what purpose?

To take over the United States? North America? The world? These madmen had to be stopped, though considering his situation at the moment, it didn't look like Tony was the man for the job.

Killian curtly addressed Tony, then lifted an Extremis inhaler from his pocket and walked toward Pepper. Tony was trapped and Pepper was in danger. He didn't think the situation could get any worse until Maya began to speak.

Maya showed Tony his old business card and reminded him that he had given it to her years ago when they were in Switzerland. On the back of the card was a formula that Tony had written. It had been smudged by their champagne, thus rendered useless. All these years later, Maya still couldn't figure it out. Now, she and Killian would make *Tony* figure it out. And if he didn't, Pepper would die. This was going to end badly, and Tony wasn't sure if he—or Iron Man—would be able to save anyone this time.

"Give us the formula," Maya pleaded. Clearly she was playing good cop to Killian's bad cop. But Tony couldn't remember it—the formula he had written left his mind long ago, long before Iron Man, and long before his panic attacks. As Maya pleaded once more, Killian grew impatient and threatened Pepper's life.

"The formula—now!" Killian demanded.

"Not going to happen," Tony said. Suddenly, an annoying beeping sound rang through the cell. One of the guards lifted Tony's pink girl's watch from his pile of confiscated items and tossed it to Killian, who grimaced at the sight. "Oh, sorry to interrupt your fantasy," Tony said. "That's just my wake-up call." Tony then turned his back on them and started count down from five hundred. The guards looked puzzled, and Killian looked annoyed.

Maya turned to Killian to ask him what he hoped to gain by this. "After tonight, I'll have the West's most powerful leader and the world's most feared terrorist. One in each pocket. Get the picture?" he said to her. "I've bought the rights to the war on terror. I am both sides by proxy. I can ratchet it up or down. Sell *my* soldiers to the fight." And that's when Maya realized that she was in way over her head. Killian wasn't interested in furthering scientific research or bettering the human condition. He was only interesting in power and control, and that made him very, very dangerous. Maya looked from Pepper to Tony, then began backing out of the cell.

Maya tried to stay calm and seemed to go back to work on one of the plants in her lab, but she actually rigged it to explode. The blast went off right behind Killian, knocking him to the ground, but it wasn't enough for Tony or Pepper—or her—to escape. Her moment of redemption had proved pointless.

Killian rose and faced Maya. He noticed the fear on her face. Then he lifted a gun from inside his jacket and fired.

"A new position has opened at A.I.M.," Killian said, bereft of humor. Then he turned to the guards and motioned to Pepper. "Bring her," he said as he started down the hallway. "Goodbye, Mister Stark," Killian called out from the opposite end of the hall. As Killian disappeared into the bowels of the basement,

Tony kept counting. It was hard for him to concentrate after what happened to Maya and Pepper, but he had to continue on. Right now, he might be the only hope the world had left.

Killian continued on through the basement. As he walked down a long corridor, the sound of scraping and scratching metal could be heard. As the sound grew louder and more intense, Killian finally saw the source of horrible noise: two Extremis guards were attempting to pry open the Iron Patriot armor. They were using crowbars, screwdrivers and hammers, but nothing worked. Rhodey was still safely inside. Savin, who was supervising the men, suggested that they use a buzzsaw to cut their way inside, but Killian didn't want them to waste their time. He ordered Savin to use his enhanced powers.

Slowly, Savin's hands began to glow and pulse with energy. When they were white-hot, Savin placed his palms on the Iron Patriot and watched as the impenetrable armor began to melt and bubble.

Killian smiled, and Rhodey felt the intense heat—and horrible pain—from inside the suit. He tolerated the unbearable pain as long as he could before finally hitting the emergency eject button.

Rhodey fell to the ground with a *thud* and was instantly surrounded by Extremis guards. They heaved him into a dirty old cell and locked the gate. From behind the rusted bars, Rhodey watched as Savin and his men took the Iron Patriot suit away. Then, turning toward Killian, he heard the evil genius radio for his helicopter. He and Pepper were heading to the docks.

On the other side of the basement, Tony was still counting down. Then, much to the guards' confusion, Tony looked up and asked them how far it was from Tennessee to Miami. The guards stared blankly at one another until suddenly, an Iron Man gauntlet came crashing through the wall. It flew onto Tony's hand just as an Iron Man boot crashed through another part of the wall. It flew onto Tony's leg. Tony struck a heroic pose, waiting for the rest of the suit, but nothing happened.

"Um, guys," Tony began, "where's the rest of you?" he asked, curious. That's when the guards attacked. But now Tony had a repulsor beam, and he wasn't afraid to use it!

Back in Rose Hill, Tennessee, Harley was hurriedly opening the other shed door. Just as he did, the rest of the Mark XLII armor came rocketing out. It flew across the sky toward Florida and Tony Stark.

Tony was dodging gunfire and firing his repulsor blast at the Extremis-enhanced A.I.M. guards. The guards had special powers and automatic weapons, so Tony was outnumbered and outgunned. And then the rest of the Iron Man armor came crashing through!

"'Bout time, boys!" Tony said as the Iron Man armor flew to him and encased him in its metal shell. For the first time in days, Tony was actually able to breathe. He felt like himself again. Using all of Iron Man's weapons, Tony quickly dispatched all of the

Extremis guards and exited his cell. He had to find Pepper.

As he searched through basement, Iron Man made his way down the long corridor, battling Extremis guards along the way. Tony was happy to be back in the suit, but the flight from Tennessee had greatly diminished the power reserves. With uncharacteristic self-control and restraint, Tony made his way through the complex, taking out guards and searching for Killian and Pepper. Tony didn't find them, but he did find Rhodey, who was locked in a cell similar to his.

"Time to go," Tony said to his longtime friend as he ripped the bars of his cell off its hinges. Rhodey told Tony that Killian had called a helicopter that was taking him and Pepper to the docks, and Tony knew that they were once again one step behind.

Neither Tony nor Rhodey was prepared to give up, but both were aware that their chances of success were declining. The Mandarin and Killian had escaped, and both villains knew by now that Iron Man and Iron Patriot were onto and after them. Now they would always be on the run; always be looking over their shoulder; always be in hiding. And Tony and Rhodey knew it, too. They would most likely not capture either madman now, but the fact that they were on the run was proof enough that Tony and Rhodey had done something right.

There was more work to be done. The Extremis guards had to be stopped, and Pepper had to be saved. It was time for action.

Tony and Rhodey made their way back to the Mandarin's compound and stole one of his speedboats. As they traveled, Rhodey used his secure line to call Vice President Rodriguez. While Rhodey was captured, he had overhead a plan of the Mandarin's to sabotage Air Force One and kill the President. Vice President Rodriguez told the Lieutenant Colonel not to worry, that he would inform the President of the attack. And the VP did just that—he wasted no time and alerted the President. The President took the warning seriously, but he wasn't worried for long. Right after he hung up the phone with the VP, the President saw Iron Patriot land a mere twenty feet from the ramp leading up to Air Force One. Now they were safe and ready to board.

But the President didn't know that it *wasn't* Lieutenant Colonel James Rhodes inside the Iron Patriot armor, but Savin. The President was walking directly into the Mandarin's ultimate trap.

CHAPTER NINETEEN

TONY AND RHODEY docked the speed-boat so that they could figure out the next part of the Mandarin's plan and how to stop it. With the Mandarin working with Killian and A.I.M.'s enhanced Extremis guards, it was not going to be easy. They needed backup. In fact, Tony was already planning for it. But first, Tony and Rhodey had to decide on their plan of attack.

With the Iron Man suit slowly gaining power, Tony decided that he would go after the President and Air Force One. Rhodey would find Pepper. He seemed to recall overhearing something about an oil tanker, and that's when Tony remembered what that bartender in Rose Hill had said about that tanker that had run aground. Tony knew it was near Miami, so the two men split up, agreeing to regroup at the tanker.

While on his way to save the President, Tony heard from JARVIS. "Sir, the cellar doors are open," the voice said to Tony, referring to the fact that emergency workers back in Malibu had finally cleared the debris away from the special cellar entrance.

Tony was elated to hear the news. "Then open the bottles and let them breathe!"

"Sir, power levels are now at ninety-two percent," JARVIS informed him. With the suit almost at full power, Tony was finally starting to feel like himself again, and finally starting to feel like he could actually take on these Extremis guards.

"Old friend," Tony said to JARVIS, "I think it's time for a party."

"The 'House Party' protocol?" JARVIS asked.

"Bring it," Iron Man answered with confidence.

Back in Malibu, a rumble was heard from the depths of what was left of Tony's mansion. Then, a circle of lights—not unlike the circle of lights around

Tony's chest—lit up from the ground. They illuminated the rubble, which seemed to come to life. Suddenly, the lights rotated as if a giant wheel or dial were turning. Then, with a mighty roar, dozens of Iron Man suits shot out of the ground and up into the sky. There were the Marks XXIII and XXVI. There was the sleek Black Stealth suit, the Deep Sea diving suit, the fortified Sub-Orbital suit, the imposing and hunched-over Heavy Lifting suit, the lightning-fast High-Velocity suit, the Silver Centurion, and many, many more.

Each of the armored suits rocketed up and banked left. They were all heading toward Tony.

CHAPTER TWENTY

BACK ON AIR FORCE ONE, Savin was ready to execute the Mandarin's plan. His mission was to exit the Iron Patriot suit, capture the President inside the armor, then place Air Force One on a collision course with the ground.

Iron Patriot rose from his chair onboard the plane and went into action. Savin took out all of the Secret Service guards first—they were no match for the Iron Patriot—then came for the President. He threw the Commander-in-Chief across the cabin with a *thud.* Savin then ejected from the armor, loaded the President in, and activated the remote-control device.

Iron Patriot—with the President trapped securely inside—crashed out of the plane and flew toward the oil tanker.

Savin strapped on a parachute and was preparing to jump when another crash rocked the plane. Looking up, Savin was now face-to-helmet with Iron Man! The Armored Avenger fired a repulsor blast at point-blank range, sending Savin sailing across the cabin. When Savin rose, ready for more, his hands were glowing and pulsing with energy.

The two traded blows and blasts. Iron Man was winning the fight until Savin decided to use the same trick that he had used on Rhodey. Savin made his hands glow extra white-hot, then placed them both on Iron Man's armor. The heat was so intense that it started to melt some of the suit and short-circuit Tony's armor.

Just then, there was another explosion inside the nose-diving plane. The force of this blast separated the two men, and when Tony looked up, he noticed that innocent people were now falling from the giant hole in the plane. Tony didn't have time for Savin now; he had to save those people. Iron Man to the rescue!

As Iron Man flew toward the first falling person, JARVIS did some quick arithmetic and calculated that there was no way for Iron Man to save everyone. He could not physically hold thirteen people, much less catch them all in time before they crashed into the water below. Tony disagreed. Iron Man increased his speed and grabbed the leg of the falling woman.

He told her that this was just like a monkey ladder and that *he* was going to fly down to each person, who would then grab the next person on the way down. Iron Man flew faster, and the woman grabbed onto a man's leg. That man then grabbed onto another man's arm, and so on. As each new "rung" was added, Tony had JARVIS send out a small electric pulse that strengthened the line. The current that ran from Iron Man down to the people made it impossible for anyone to let go or fall into the ocean. And one by one, Iron Man saved them all! He landed them in the harbor, where they could get to safety.

But Tony's armor had been through too much. His suit would have to be repaired if he were to face off against any Extremis guards. Once again, Tony was on his own, without his armor to project him. One step forward, two steps back, he thought . . .

CHAPTER TWENTY-ONE

IT WAS CHRISTMAS EVE at last. As kids anxiously awaited the arrival of Santa Claus in just a few hours, the Mandarin was preparing one final video message for the free world. As people turned on their televisions, hoping to catch glimpses of the Yule Log or their favorite Christmas story, they instead saw the Mandarin. He was on every channel, and he was addressing the country.

"My fellow Americans," the villain began, "today's lesson is to embrace change. Evolve. You might know someone with a birthday on September eleventh. Ask them how joyous their celebration ever gets. Not the same these days, never will be," the villain said, speaking truthfully, or so it seemed. "So now, and forever, enjoy December twenty-fifth, America, not as the loving holiday, but as the day your loving President was destroyed inside a red, white, and blue tin suit!" The Mandarin then began an eerie rendition of "Deck the Halls" as the camera cut to President Ellis.

The President—who was still in the Iron Patriot suit, but with the suit's visor up so that the world could see his face—was suspended forty feet above the Roxxon Norco oil tanker. He was held up by thick chains fastened to his arms and legs. Beneath him were hundreds of barrels of oil. The Mandarin's plan was to ignite the oil drums, then cut the chains so that the President would fall to a fiery grave. Tony and Rhodey would have to act fast!

Rhodey sat on the docks across from the giant tanker. From his vantage point, he saw his Iron Patriot armor land and the Extremis guards hoist the President into the air. Rhodey took in everything: how many guards there were; exit points on and off the boat; spots to dive for cover. He also took notice of who *wasn't* there: Killian. Of course *he* wouldn't be there, Rhodey thought. Why would Killian chance being caught? No, neither villain would be there, but an example still had to be made, and the enemy still had to be defeated.

When Tony joined him, the two decided to scale the side of the tanker by climbing up the long mooring ropes. Once onboard, Rhodey would go after the President, and Tony would go after Savin and rescue Pepper.

Tony and Rhodey made their way onto the boat, but they were soon discovered by the Extremis guards, who launched an all-out attack. Rhodey and Tony were losing. Then they noticed the oil drums. They kicked over a few, and the gunfire from the guards ignited the oil, creating a wall of fire around the Extremis guards. Tony and Rhodey thought they were safe—until the enhanced guards simply walked through the fire or regenerated from it. They needed reinforcements, and fast. Again, as if on cue, the cavalry arrived.

There was an intense buzzing in the air and a sudden breeze as if from nowhere. One by one, Tony,

Rhodey, and all of the guards looked up to see themselves surrounded by thirty different Iron Man suits of armor. The various suits encircled the tanker and began to lower themselves in formation. It was an impressive and awe-inspiring sight. And now, it was also a fair fight.

"Well, what are you waiting for?" Tony yelled out. "It's Christmas—take 'em to church!" And with that battle cry, the suits of armor went into action.

The Deep Sea suit lunged at a guard, and the two fell off the tanker and into the sea, where the suit, which Tony called Hammerhead, would have its greatest advantage.

The Heavy Lifting armor, called Igor because of it massive upper body and hunched appearance, took on three guards at once. Even three super-powered Extremis guards didn't equal the strength of this monster, which took them down with ease.

The same was true of the Black Stealth suit, which Tony called Nightclub. It snuck up on guards and took them out. Then the Disaster Rescue Suit, nicknamed

Red Snapper, used its pincer-like claws to grab the guards. But not all suits were so lucky. Some of them were damaged beyond repair, and some were treated as if they were tinker toys in the Extremis guards' hands.

Repulsor blasts, miniature missiles, beams of glowing Extremis energy, and a barrage of bullets zigzagged across the tanker as explosions rang out. The battle raged on as Rhodey began scaling the ship. If he could get to President Ellis, he could free him and join the fight as Iron Patriot, and right now, they needed all the help they could get. It was a slow and dangerous climb, but Rhodey was determined.

On the main deck, Tony continued to battle the Extremis guards as his suits continued their own fights. Both the Skeleton armor and the Silver Centurion armor fired enough blasts to give Tony cover. He charged forward and fired off a series of quick, powerful repulsor beams. With each Extremis guard who fell, Tony was getting closer and closer to finding Pepper. But just when Tony was in between suits, Brandt attacked.

The Iron Man armor at Tony's feet was heavily damaged. It was sparking and shorting out, and there was no way Tony could use it to battle Brandt. Gone was the woman who briefly flirted with him outside the Walker's Bar. In her place was a vicious killing machine that was determined to destroy Tony Stark.

With no place left for Tony to run, Brandt charged at him and lifted him into the air with her left hand. Then her right hand began to glow. It pulsed with energy until it was white-hot. But just as Brandt was about to deliver the killing blow, something knocked her down—hard. No, not some*thing*—some*one*. Pepper Potts appeared before the two of them, exhausted from having charged into Brandt at full force. Tony stood staring at Pepper, thankful that she was alive, and thankful that she saved him.

Before the two could speak, Brandt was back on her feet and charging at Pepper. As a rogue Iron Man suit joined the battle, Pepper grabbed an Iron Man gauntlet from one of Tony's destroyed suits and put it on her hand. As Brandt reared back, Pepper let loose a mighty repulsor blast from the gauntlet. It knocked Brandt across the ship and over the edge, where she was swallowed by the Atlantic.

Pepper looked at the gauntlet on her hand and dropped it to the ground. Then she looked up at Tony with tears in her eyes. He ran to her and the two embraced. "It's okay, it's okay," he said quietly. But they didn't have time for a reunion. Tony had to keep fighting.

Forty feet above the main deck, Rhodey was about to do his best Tarzan impression and swing from a chain. Holding his gun in his hand, Rhodey took a leap of faith and swung toward the President. As he did, he fired with expert precision at the chains holding up the President. *Snap! Snap! Snap! Snap!* The gunfire had done the trick. As the chains broke, the Iron Patriot suit—with the President still inside—began to fall toward a lower level. At the same time, Rhodey let go of his chain and fell on top of the suit.

Rhodey commanded the suit to open, and it ejected President Ellis and encased James Rhodes.

Now Iron Patriot once more, Rhodey grabbed the President and flew him away from the tanker to safety. Then Rhodey fired his boosters and flew back to join Tony onboard the tanker.

Back on the ship, Tony and his Iron Man suits were making progress. But there was one man standing in his way; one more man who had to be defeated before the rest of the Extremis guards would surrender: Savin.

Tony stood opposite Savin, whose arms began to glow and pulse. Tony jumped and lunged out of the way of Savin's attacks. He just had to hang on a little bit longer. Unbeknownst to Savin, Tony was instructing the Mark XLII armor to him, but when it arrived, Tony saw that it had been heavily damaged. They encircled him and eventually encased him. The villain was now wearing the Iron Man armor.

Savin laughed at Tony Stark. As if he weren't powerful enough with the Extremis Code, he was now in possession of his own Iron Man armor. He advanced toward Tony with an evil grin under the Iron Man helmet. Then Tony dived behind some metal casing and yelled to JARVIS.

"Blow the suit!" Tony screamed. By the time Savin realized what was going on, it was too late. JARVIS followed Tony's order and engaged the self-destruct on the Mark XLII. The suit erupted in a massive explosion, completely destroying it—and Savin.

As the smoke cleared, Tony rose and surveyed the scene. Around him were bits and pieces of his various Iron Man suits of armor, all of which had been badly damaged in the battle. Extremis guards were strewn about the deck, and others were holding their hands up in surrender. The battle was finally over. The good guys had finally won. It was a Christmas miracle!

Tony and Pepper embraced, and as Iron Patriot joined the two of them on the deck, the trio looked out across the ocean. This had been their most dangerous adventure yet, one that had cost Tony his suits of armor and his home, but none of that mattered to him now. He had saved what mattered most: his friends. He also saved the free world from the clutches of the Mandarin. Tony knew that he hadn't seen the end of him—or Killian—but he also knew that they wouldn't return any time soon. They wouldn't dare.

For the first time in a long while, Tony breathed easy and smiled.

CHAPTER TWENTY-TWO

A FEW DAYS LATER, Tony Stark stood inside Happy's hospital room. He had come to visit Happy, though after the events of the past week, it looked as if Tony should be the one lying in the hospital bed.

Tony leaned over his longtime friend and began to speak to him. "So maybe it ends here, or maybe it just begins again. The circle of life, right? Just like *The Lion King*," he said. But Tony wasn't referring to Happy—he knew his friend was on the mend. He was referring to himself. It was time for Tony to decide how he would go forward, and how he would live. Would he continue to be dependent on his Iron Man armor and persona? Would his panic attacks continue? Or would he move on and begin again, just like Simba?

Tony thought long and hard about everything that had happened to him, from when the shrapnel first hit his heart and he began Iron Man to his most recent battle in Florida against the Mandarin and the Extremis guards. Then he took a deep breath and smiled. He had made up his mind.

"See, it turns out that Iron Man wasn't a home, and it wasn't a shell. It was a cocoon," he said aloud. "And now, I'm a changed man."

Tony beamed with pride. "I'm Tony Stark."

The End.

EPILOGUE

INSIDE HIS SECRET LAIR, the Mandarin pounded his fists on the table before him. He had wired the tanker with miniature cameras and had been watching the events unfold before him in real time. He had been defeated. The promise of enhanced humans with extraordinary powers had been no match for Iron Man and his suits of armor.

The Mandarin had clearly underestimated Tony Stark. That was not a mistake he would ever make again. Even if it took him years to rebuild his empire and gather new resources and men, the Mandarin would have his revenge on Iron Man. He swore it.

* * *

It was New Year's Eve in Rose Hill, Tennessee, and Harley went to get a tool out of his father's shed. He approached the ramshackle door, and when he opened it, his jaw almost hit the floor. Gone was the dirty old workbench, the rusty tools, and the drafty wooden boards. In their place was a brand-new, high-tech interior tricked out with state-of-the-art computers and electronics. Harley smiled from ear to ear. Tony Stark was his hero!

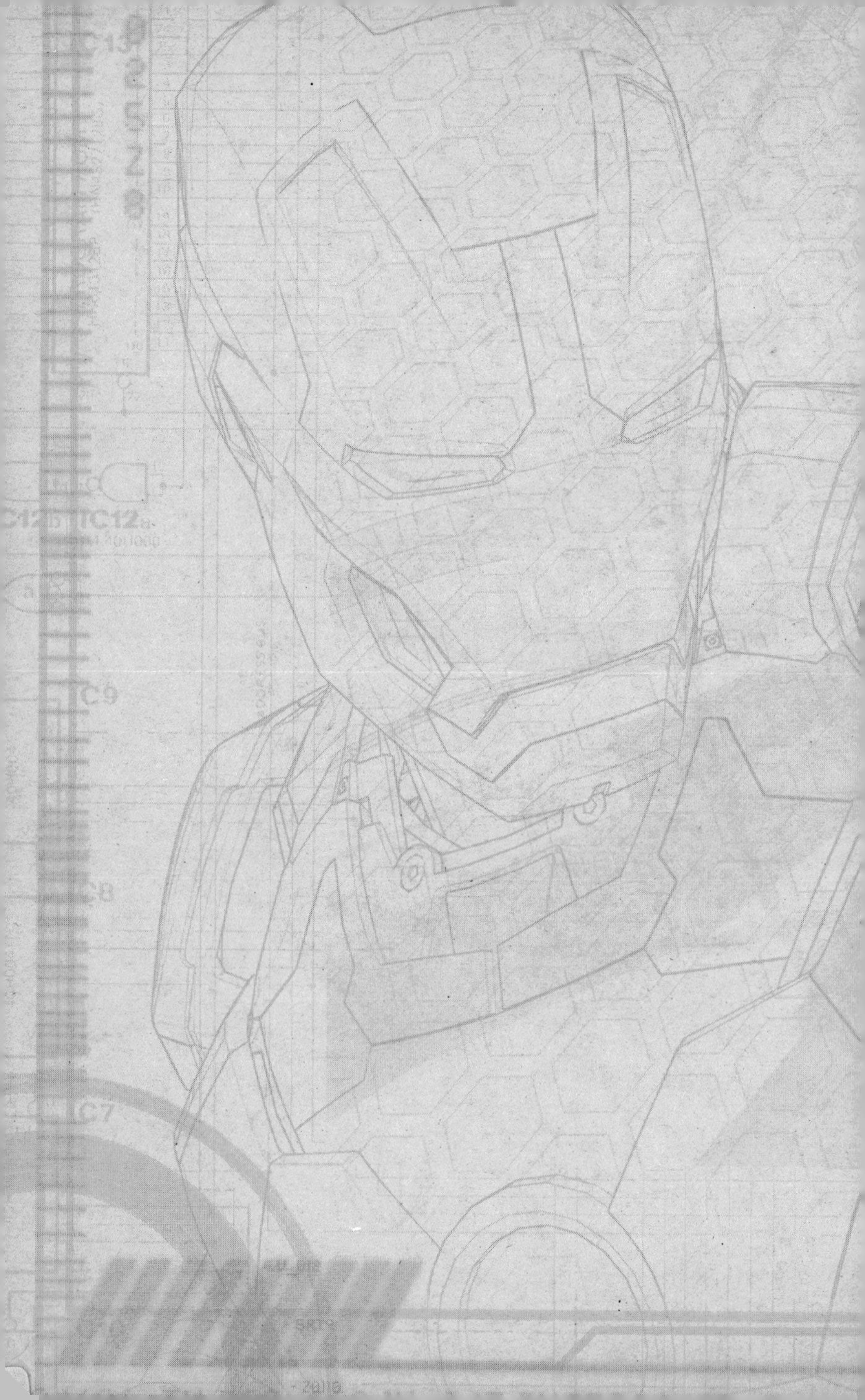
C9
C8
C7